WORKBOOK PRESS LLC
187 E Warm Springs Rd,
Suite B285, Las Vegas, NV 89119, USA

Website: https://workbookpress.com/
Hotline: 1-888-818-4856
Email: admin@workbookpress.com

Ordering Information:
Quantity sales. Special discounts are available on quantity purchases by corporations, associations, and others.
For details, contact the publisher at the address above.

Library of Congress Control Number:

ISBN-13:   000-0-000000-00-0 (Paperback Version)
                000-0-000000-00-0 (Digital Version)

REV. DATE: 05/07/2022

THE OLD LIGHTHOUSE

by

E. Thornton Goode, Jr.

IN APPRECIATION

To Mrs. Bettie Brakebill, my 10th and 11th grade English teacher, who thought enough of this work to do the editing, and encouraged me to send it for publication.

And to my Mom and Dad, Marilyn and Gene, my Sister, Catherine, and my Youngest Brother, Robert, for their unwavering support, both emotionally and financially regarding all my sometimes outlandish endeavors.

PROLOGUE

The world has basically been defined in the three dimensions of height, width and length. However, none of this reality could exist without the fourth dimension of time. The only reason we perceive all physical things is because of time. With the physical comes the philosophical world and life. And with human life, there is emotion. Emotions allow friendship and possibly love.

Time goes on to infinity. Even without a clock, time is ticking away. Is it possible that as time moves forward, so do life and love, never ending? What are the consequences of these never ending factors, touching each and every one of us, sometimes in strange and different ways? This is the subject of our story.

CHAPTER I

I hated God and what He did. What was the reason? Why was I part of His cruel game? Why did my life have to get torn apart?

Alone, I stood looking out at the ruins of the old lighthouse. For a moment, I closed my eyes and in my mind saw the storm raging as if it were yesterday. The horror and terror of it flashed a chill through my body. The stinging sensations of the beating rain still seemed to linger on my face. I quickly opened my eyes.

My mind was very logical and could accept what my ears heard and my eyes saw, the things that were real. But my heart was a maverick. Even with all the bleeding and pain, tearing my heart apart, these facts would not be acknowledged. The unreal had embraced my every emotion, leaving memories that would last all eternity.

My head tilted back as I closed my eyes. My whole body constricted with frustration. My fists clinched. I drew a deep breath, and my entire being shook with tension.

"WHY ME?…I DON'T DESERVE THIS!…WHY ME?" My words resounded into the gentle sea breeze.

I opened my eyes, then sat on a nearby rock. All the questions I had whirled through me like a thousand pieces of a puzzle, caught in the vortex of a tornado. Would I be able to put it all together and save myself?

In college, I had been an art major, not a psychology or science major. I deal with the unreal when placing paint on a canvas. I extract images from reality or create fantasies putting them on canvas to make them seem real.

But how could my heart come to grips having known the alive, the substance, the emotions, only to be told that none of these things could have been real? This was beyond my comprehension.

The rays of the mid-September sun were warm, but the cool breeze made me aware of the tears running down my cheeks. I wiped my face with my left hand and spoke softly. "God! What about me? It's not fair! It's just not fair!"

I bit down hard on my lower lip in an effort to rid myself of the painful lump, deep in my chest. I thought I would surely die if the agony inside me became worse.

I looked out at the lighthouse again. I could see it clearly. There was no doubt the physical structure was real and in my mind was the only tangible object joining the real to the unreal. The lighthouse had to be the key to the entire puzzle. I guess that's why I came, hoping I would find an answer. I was sure the answer would be there.

I slowly rubbed my hand over the rock where I sat. Through my sadness, a little chuckle and smile came to me when I realized this rock and I were old friends. It was the same one on which I used to sit and wait for Daniel.

The sound of the surf breaking on the nearby rocks was mesmerizing. I began to fall into a trance, recalling my first encounter with this location. I smiled with mixed emotions at the reverie creeping into my mind. Everything began a little more than three months ago, in early summer.

CHAPTER II

It had taken me several months, but finally I'd made my decision. Several factors, especially money, played a big roll in choosing this small seaside town. Another factor was the reality of the place. True colors and visuals made it unnecessary to imagine the scenes. This whole area of the upper East Coast was secluded and off the beaten path. No screaming beach crowds were here. But that's what I wanted. Painting with critics hanging over your shoulder is not very conducive to creativity. And after all, the sound of the surf was so relaxing.

Early June was upon me and I felt I had all the time in the world. It was going to be a wonderful three months of nothing but painting. I didn't have a care in the world. September would come soon enough. That's when I would go home and back to my life in the city.

Having been here almost a week, I'd seen numerous places with great potential for a painting. Now here I was on the beach, some fifteen miles from town and my painting was coming along quite well. This was the second day out here and I'd seen not one person the whole time. I parked the car some distance from this spot. Trekking a distance was preferable to getting the car stuck to the axles in sand. I couldn't even see it from where I was. Theft was of no concern. The car was a clunker and not worth stealing.

After applying some phthalo green to the canvas, I stuck the end of the handle of the half-inch wide artist's brush in my mouth, a habit of mine for as long as I could remember. My mouth was always a good place to hold a brush when I needed my right hand free so I could scratch my head. With the palette in my left hand, I stood there looking at the canvas, virtually finished. I needed to step back so I could compare the painting to the actual scene. Continuing to look at the canvas, I started backing up.

The sand was cool and damp under my bare feet. It felt good to have the tiny grains scrunch through my toes. The only interruptions were from a lonely seagull flying by, screeching his criticism of my work. But what did he know?

Slowly retreating from the canvas, I could see the colors were perfect. The beiges, browns and ochers depicted the reality of the sand dunes covered with the wind blown grasses and sea oats, the pounding surf of blues and greens to the left of the dunes, and the hint of the old lighthouse, graying in the distance.

That will be the next painting, I thought, as my eyes lingered, looking in the direction of the lighthouse located some two miles down the beach. My mind must have gone into some short trance pondering the old structure and wondered of its history. Suddenly, I caught myself and returned to the subject at hand.

My eyes returned to the painting. I needed to back up further, to imagine the painting on a wall. Retreating six more steps, the brush still in my mouth, I smiled at my accomplishment. It was a good painting. "To hell with the seagull." I laughed.

I was enjoying myself. There was nothing like being there, in person. The breeze blowing my hair a mess, the sound of the roaring, crashing waves, the smell of the sea, the sand under my feet. To paint from reality instead of my imagination was always my preference but wasn't always feasible. Reveling in my pleasure, I found myself whistling Rachmininoff's Eighteenth Variation, one of my favorite pieces of classical music.

Without warning, from behind and above my right shoulder came a deep, stable masculine voice. "You're damn good!"

The sound was unexpected. Rather rattled, I clumsily turned in a clockwise motion. The bristles of the brush, I was holding in my mouth, moved from left to right on one of the wide white bands that alternated with red. In my turn, I lost my balance. His strong hand reached out and grabbed my right arm, but not in time to prevent the swing of my left arm, the one holding the palette. It landed on the field of alternating red and white bands.

In a few moments, I regained my balance and pulled the palette away. My eyes went immediately to the mess of white, browns, ochers, yellows, blues, greens, all splotched across the lower right area of his shirt. The streak of phthalo green was almost in the middle of the white band, crossing his broad chest. I stepped back two steps.

A barefooted giant was standing in front of me, and his shadow eclipsed the sun. It took me a minute to see his entire image. The shirt fit his torso well. Because it had short sleeves and his pants were cut off, his muscular body was easily seen. His well-tanned skin was covered with dark hair.

A captain's hat covered most of his black wavy hair, which was slightly graying at the temples. A black mustache, extending beyond the corners of his mouth accentuated his strong jaw line. He seemed to be a few years older than myself. He was a very handsome man.

I peered into his face. That's when I saw them, slightly shaded by the visor of the hat and his black eyebrows. His eyes were blue, an incredible blue. I'd never seen eyes like that before in my whole life. They held a look of disaster and terror, cold as a blue berg. I felt as doomed as the ill-fated Titanic. For my clumsiness, I knew I was going to die.

But then, those eyes became warm, like the shining waters of a tropical lagoon at sunset, calm and inviting. I stood like a statue; his eyes still riveted to mine. Instantly, I gathered my wits seeing clearly the now ruined shirt. "I'm sorry! I lost my balance! I promise I'll replace your shirt!"

At that moment, the titan's stern expression changed. His mouth formed a smile, growing bigger and bigger. Then he spoke. His voice was clear and calm, as if nothing had happened. "My fault. Shouldn't have startled you . . . And don't worry about the shirt. I'll keep it. Maybe you're a famous artist. Shirt will really be worth something." He began to laugh.

I began to relax somewhat, knowing I wasn't going to be pulverized, smashed into the sand or thrown into the ocean. I tried to cover my nervousness with a chuckle. "No, seriously! I WILL replace your shirt."

Seeming to forget the instant past, he turned, examining the canvas. "Gotta tell ya. Good work. Damn good work. Must make a lot of money."

"Well, I wouldn't go that far." I was honest in my modesty.

"Got any more? Sure would like to see more. Bet they're just as pretty." He looked back at me again.

I could see his white teeth through the slightly separated smile. "Well, I have a few things back at the boarding house where I'm staying in town. If you'd like, why don't you drop by later on?"

He glanced down at the sand, then back up at me again. There was a slight look of embarrassment. "Well, you see, I live at the lighthouse and getting to town is a bit of a walk." But his expression quickly changed. He smiled wide. "Seems you have a way to get back and forth. Maybe you could come back later, to the lighthouse, and visit . . . Have dinner and all? Caught some nice fish today. Mom taught me to cook real well."

I pondered the invitation a second. "Oh why not! I think it would be great fun to see a real lighthouse. I've always wondered how they worked . . . and I'll bring a few of my paintings."

"It's a trade. You show me your pictures and I'll show you how a lighthouse works."

"How does seven-thirty sound?"

"Seven-thirty? Great! . . . Be lookin' forward to seeing you then." It looked as if his whole being was exploding with joy, like I was someone special, coming for a visit. His face beamed. He quickly smiled, winked his left eye, then turned and jogged off in the direction of the lighthouse. In a moment, he disappeared behind a sand dune.

A smile was on my face as I watched him go. "Nice guy." Then it dawned on me. I don't know his name! I'm having dinner with someone I don't even know. I shook my head and laughed. The joke is on us both. He doesn't know my name either.

I removed the canvas from the easel, and headed for the car. It took two more trips to get the rest of my art supplies and other related items. All the while, I kept thinking about the "Blue Eyed Captain." Why would someone who looked like him, stash himself away in an old lighthouse, way out here beyond civilization? There was nothing out here except the sand, the surf, the breeze, the dunes, the quiet, the solitude, the peace. I stopped and laughed. That's why I came to this area for the summer. But to live? Don't think I could go that far. He must really love it here.

Getting in my car, I started driving back to town. The narrow asphalt road was one lane wide and covered with patches of sand that had blown over it. It was obvious this road was not often traveled. After some two miles, the road dead-ended on to a two lane coastal highway, where there was little sign of habitation until a few miles south of town. Dwellings, typical of rental and seasonal occupancy, dotted the roadside. No major building over three stories high constituted the main part of town. The older structures were of brick and stone lining the main street. Many of these had been renovated into shops and some into bed and breakfast establishments as well as interesting eateries. There, too, were several churches, representing a few of the major local religious institutions. Any indication that this town was once a thriving and important shipping and trading center was left up only to one's imagination and the town history.

Driving almost to the center of town, I turned left to a side street. After several blocks and a few more turns on to lesser lanes, I came to the boarding house where I had rented a room for the summer. The two story wooden building had once been a large single-family house, now divided into several segregated rooms. Mine was in the back of the house accessible by its own entrance.

During the entire drive back, I thought of the man who startled me at the beach. Little did I realize this encounter would be the beginning of a bizarre twist of fate, affecting my entire life. There was no way I could have known how events were going to unfold and what was going to happen. If only I could have changed it.

CHAPTER III

What could I say? My accommodations were drab. But what was I to expect with what I could afford? That's why I had brought several of my paintings to hang on the walls. They added color, if nothing else. Actually, it wasn't as bad as I've made it sound. The rooms were clean and neat.

I walked in, took the five paintings off the walls and took them to the car. Putting them in the back seat, I thought it would be interesting to hear his comments on them. Then I realized. How egotistical can you get? He might not like them. After all, they are mountain and meadow scenes, and he likes the sea.

I took a shower, shaved, trimmed my mustache, then splashed myself with cologne. Setting the bottle down, I saw the blue sailing ship on the ivory colored bottle reflected in the mirror over the sink. I laughed. How appropriate . . . the sand, ocean, lighthouse and all.

After dressing, I went into the kitchen area. From the cabinet, I pulled out the decanter of gin and also the bottle of Chardonnay I was keeping for some special occasion. It would be appropriate since he was having fish. I popped them in a paper bag, then started out the door. At that moment, my eyes saw the pair of binoculars sitting on the counter. I went and grabbed them up thinking they would be useful to see far out to sea from the top of the lighthouse. Swinging the strap over my head, I headed for the car.

On the way, I stopped by the gallery/art supply shop to get a few tubes of paint and talk with Bob Williams, the owner and manager. Bob was one of those who has never known an enemy. Easy going and talkative, in a quiet manner, it was evident from the start he was extremely knowledgeable of his profession. His blond hair was slightly balding and his gray eyes reminded me of some of the interesting marbles I use to have as a kid.

When he found out I painted, he was quick to give me some information on the art show to be judged at the end of the summer, in early September. He asked, then virtually insisted that I enter a couple of my works. I smiled and indicated I would consider it knowing it would be good promotion for me.

"Important clients usually come to see the works after the critics give their awards. The paintings remain on display for at least a month, before being returned to the artists or their owners, if they'd been sold. I must say that the ones done by the winners usually command pretty high prices and could mean potential future sales and commissions."

"Bob, I'll try to have two entries for the show. How's that?"

He smiled and placed his hands together in and washing motion. "Good. I'll look forward to seeing them as soon as you can get them finished."

The next stop was the small market to pick up a bottle of tonic and a lime for my gin. I didn't know what it was about small markets verses the big city super grocery store, but I really liked them. Maybe it was that inner desire for a reach back to a more simplistic and less hectic time.

Leaving the market, I headed south, out of town, down the coastal highway toward the old lighthouse. I retraced the way I had earlier on to the side road and passed the place I had stopped to paint earlier in the day. I was now in new territory, having never driven out that far. I could see the top of the lighthouse tower over the dunes. It looked to be some mile and a half away. At that point, the asphalt surface of the road ended and a shell and sand surface started.

"My old tires are not going to forgive me for this torture. If I don't have a blow out, it will be amazing." I shook my head, squinted my eyes and winced, just waiting for some thing to happen.

The road finally ended and I couldn't go any further with the car. Ahead of me was just sand. I could see the light was still some quarter mile away. The top of it was visible above the mountains of sand. I parked the car at the end of the hard shell surface, right at the foot of a huge dune. I could no longer see the lighthouse. Putting the binoculars around my neck and grabbing several items, I walked through the valleys between the dunes, in the direction of the light. I'd come back for the paintings on the next trip.

As I rounded the last dune, the beach sloped down to a rocky shore. I stopped in my tracks. There was the light, about a hundred yards out on a small island. I was stunned at first, wondering how I was to get there. But then, I felt a warmth inside telling me not to worry. I just smiled, then set everything down on the sand. I ran back to the car to get the paintings.

When I returned, I really took the time to see the wonderful visual at hand. The setting sun gave a golden glow to the scene. It was beautiful, like something out of a romance novel. The tall, round, stone lighthouse loomed above the attached stone cottage. Even at the distance, I could tell the roof of the cottage was of slate, from its texture and blue-gray color. The scene was so quaint, unreal, picturesque.

At that moment, I saw a figure come out of the front door of the cottage. He must have been periodically checking the beach to see when I would arrive. He waved then started jogging down what I would come to find was the long flight of stone steps leading to the small sandy beach below, where the small skiff was moored. Soon the skiff was out in the waves. I raised the binoculars to see his powerful arms pulling at the oars, plunging the boat through the water with the ease of a hot knife through warm butter. His back was to me until he landed.

Jumping to the sand, he walked toward me. The cap he wore was still on his head. The visor gave no shadow this time because the sun was low in the western sky. I could see his face fully. He had a big grin and his eyes glinted like beacons in the golden light. I noticed that his feet were still bare, but he no longer wore the shirt with my paint splatters on the front. This shirt was rather bulky and made of rough linen. He thrust his right hand at me. "Daniel Coffin . . . Sorry I didn't say it before. Don't know why. Call me Dan."

I thought my hand would be crushed as I shook his. "James, Jim Jefferies. Nice to meet you, Dan . . . again." The pressure of his hand caused me to wince, but even in slight pain, I grinned.

He eased up. "Sorry. Sometimes I don't know my own strength. Glad ya came, Jim. Let's get these beautiful things over to the house." He reached down with his huge hands, and with the care, as if picking up a baby, placed the paintings in the bottom of the boat. "Jump in and we'll be off."

I climbed in and sat in the rear of the skiff. Daniel pushed the bow into deeper water before jumping in. He grabbed the oars and we were into the waves.

The waves were not like those on the open beach, their power diminished by the many large rocks projecting from below the swirling blue-green. The surf crashed on them, sending sprays of foam high into the air, picking up the orange tinted light from the sun.

Without realizing, I spoke out loud. "God! This is so beautiful."

"Yeah, I know. Don't think there's anyone who appreciates this place like I do. Guess that's why I never left." His voice had a touch of laughter in it.

His response answered part of my question about him. There was much to be discovered concerning this man called Daniel Coffin, but in good time. I had the whole summer to talk with him since it was obvious he wasn't going anywhere.

Before long, we were on the small beach area of the island.

Gathering the things from the boat, we headed up the flight of stone steps to the cottage.

The light tower and cottage were nestled in the rocks, some thirty feet above the sea. Wild summer flowers of pinks, reds and yellows, with infrequent splashes of blue and violet, graced almost every nook in the rocks, cascading over and down like permanent waves of color. Clumps of green grasses, brown sea oats and wind swept scrub brush stuck here and there, seemed to give a finishing touch. Unlike the dynamic waters below, the natural plantings gave a softness to the texture of the whole scene.

Daniel was leading the way when we reached the entry. He turned to me. I'd never witnessed such genuine warmth in an individual before. He seemed to radiate happiness. "Jim, welcome to my house." He opened the wooden door, ducking to keep from hitting the top of the frame, and walked in.

As I entered, I stood there, looking around. I felt I had walked into another world, one of a bygone era. Two steps in front of me led down into a large vaulted room. Although the walls were the same exterior gray stone and wood planking of a natural gray-beige, the whole, overall feeling of the interior was warm. Oriental type rugs of simple design covered several areas of the black-gray flagstone flooring. Large hand hewn beams supporting the roof were arranged in an open design, allowing a view of the loft area above, accessible by an open wooden stair on the right.

Heavy drapes of dark green velvet were tied back from the few windows that pierced the thick exterior walls. I was sure this heavy construction was intended not only to prevent the excessive loss of heat in the winter months, but also to withstand storm winds from the sea.

Light from the candles, oil lamps and the fireplace at the far end of the room gave a warmth to the atmosphere as well as an amber cast to everything. Electricity was non-existent on the island. There was a ten-candle chandelier suspended from the roof structural beams on a pulley so it could be lowered and raised. An eight-candle one hung over the table in the dining area, to my left.

The room seemed to be full of antiques. Many decorative items were oriented toward ships, possibly from shipwrecks up and down the beach. An unexpected surprise was the presence of a small grand piano in the far-left corner of the main room. Along the wall with the fireplace and the interior wall to the right were shelves and shelves of books. Daniel somehow had accumulated a substantial small library.

My ears were filled with the sound of a music box. Not just any music box, but a music box of music boxes. It was one of the old metal disk type, that you can change. It was playing Bach's Cantata 147, 'Jesu, Joy of Man's Desiring'. The melodic tones resounded through the space.

Continuing to peruse the room, I saw many beautiful shells and several items of glass. These flat panes, colored bottles and drinking glasses were engraved with intricate patterns and designs. I'd seen a lot of good cut glass but these pieces were true collector items. I picked up a large goblet, examining the cutwork. "This is absolutely stunning. Don't see much of this any more, except in fine shops and museums. Where did you get it?"

Daniel had placed the paintings by the settee and had gone to the fireplace. He needed to shift the logs to perk up the flames. Responding to my question, he turned to see what I was talking about. Quickly, his expression became that of a child being praised for an extra special deed well done. His voice was quiet. "Thanks. I did that."

"You did THIS?" I turned staring directly at him and sounding like a maniac in disbelief. My mind was trying to fathom those huge hands doing such delicate work.

The look on his face seemed to be asking why I thought he would lie. "Yeah. I do it in spare time, or when I'm watching the light."

I placed the goblet back on the table. "I AM impressed!"

I stood in awe of the coziness and the interior's simplistic elegance. Everything fit. The warmth did not overshadow his masculinity. I would eventually find out the interior reflected the man in many ways.

Then I looked at my landscapes by the settee. Bet they'd look great on the walls, I thought, seeing empty spaces where two of them might fit. The bright colors of the paintings could only enhance the room. I said nothing.

Daniel finished adjusting the logs. "Let's finish seeing the rest of the house."

I followed him down a narrow hall to the right of the fireplace. There were three doors in front of us. One was on the left, just a few feet down the hall. The next was on the right. The last was at the very end of the hall. He opened the door on the right and we entered a small room that I discovered later, backed up to the kitchen. There was a cabinet with a large mirror over it and a large porcelain bowl and pitcher sitting on it. Toiletry items were assembled near the bowl. The tub was one of those old 'Ball and Claw' types, but had no fixtures. I was sure the water had to be brought in and heated on the stove or in the fireplace. But what did I expect? The whole house was a true relic. A small fireplace, used to heat the room on cold days, shared the same stone chimney with the kitchen.

Then I thought of the stove in the kitchen. Bet it's a wood burner and made the year Jesus was born. Probably why Daniel uses the fireplace so much. No need to have two fires going in the summer.

The second door down the hall opened to a very small room. This was the out house, but accessible from indoors. Daniel would explain later that he did not swim on this side of the island, since there was possible contamination where everything ran down to the water. He indicated that once a week or more he poured a few buckets of water into the hole to wash away anything seeming to collect below. I noticed that the door fit well. I was sure it was a cold duty in the wintertime.

"That door leads to the light." Daniel pointed to the last door at the end of the hall. "We'll be going up there later."

We retraced our steps and went through a door in the interior wooden wall, right at the foot of the staircase. It was the entry to the kitchen. My mental concept of the stove was correct. The floor was of the same flagstone. All the cabinets were of rough-cut wood that had been white washed. Even the counter tops were wood. The metal sink had no fixtures, only a drain.

When we returned to the living room, I went over and opened one of the bags I'd set on the breakfront. I pulled out the bottle of wine, waving it in the air. "You might wanna keep this cold."

"Good idea!" Daniel took the bottle and went out the front door. Momentarily, he returned, without it.

By that time, I had my decanter of gin on the breakfront. "How about a drink?"

Daniel was back at the fire again. "Sure. I've got some whisky up there in the breakfront along with some glasses."

I opened the double doors, each set with leaded glass, diamond shaped panes. Many of the clear panes were cut with exquisite floral designs. On the shelf in front of me was a set of goblets. The cutwork on all of them was the same, except one. It had his name on it, surrounded with many swirling vines and leaves. I took it down. These must be some of the other pieces he has done. The work was that of a true artisan. I held up the one with his name on it and another similar to it. "These okay?"

He turned to look. "Right!"

A single decanter stood next to the set of glasses. It, too, was a work of art, covered with vines and leaves, undulating around a three-masted, eighteenth century ship, in full sail. The detail work of etching and cutting was astounding. I took it down and poured his glass half full. I placed the decanter beside the ones I had brought. I laughed to myself in the comparison. Store bought just can't touch the real thing. I poured some gin in the other glass.

All of a sudden, without thinking, I blurted something stupid and insensitive. "Where's the ice?" Hearing the words, I thought my tongue should have been torn out. I felt like crawling under one of the stones in the floor. How could I not remember the obvious? There couldn't possibly be any ice. There's no electricity, no refrigerator.

Daniel had finished at the fire and was walking my way. "Sure!" He grabbed the two glasses and went out the front door again. Soon he was back with a few chunks of ice in each glass. He handed me the one with the gin, then returned to the fire.

"Thanks!" I added the tonic to my glass, glad in the fact my blunder had no foundation. I was not sure of the source for the ice, but I didn't want to question anymore. The embarrassment I experienced was quickly gone. In the time ahead, we would laugh heartily when I shared this incident with Daniel.

"I need a knife to cut my lime." I picked a big green lime from the grocery bag.

"In the drawer by the sink." Daniel yelled.

Easily finding the knife exactly where he said it was, I returned to the breakfront. I cut the lime and squeezed it in my glass. After a quick stir, I took a sip to test it. It was perfect. I walked over to the piano bench and sat down.

The music box was winding down. Daniel went over, removed the metal disk, and placed it in the cabinet under the music box. He pulled out another and set it on the spindle. After a few cranks, the strains of Mozart filled the room.

He walked over to the canvases, leaning up against the settee and end table. "Jim, these are damn good." He took a sip of his drink, continuing his careful examination. "I like how you made the mountains. They're so colorful. I've seen hills around here, but never any real mountains. Haven't traveled that much. Have to admit they look so powerful and majestic. You've obviously been there."

"Yeah, a few years ago. Took a little artist's license, but that's okay. Most of it's from the real thing."

He sat on the floor in front of the paintings for some time looking at the scenes. Finally, he commented. "I feel like I could get up and walk right into them. They really are beautiful, so real."

I'd made myself comfortable at the piano and leaned back against the keyboard, looking up through the entire house. Suddenly, I was just talking out loud. "Daniel, you have so many lovely things."

Daniel stopped his perusal of my work for a moment. "Dad used to bring Mom lots of things when he'd come home from his trips. Some of the other stuff's from wrecks along the coast." He paused for a moment. "Every once in a while the damn light goes out and gettin' it started again is a real bitch . . . And sometimes there's no oil. That's when it's really frustrating because you can't do a damn thing." After another slight pause he began again. "Dad was constantly bringing books home for Mom and I to read. He always said that you could find anything in books."

He stopped looking at the paintings and walked over to the fireplace. Using the tongs from the hearth, he pulled out the iron pot that was hanging on the bracket, then set it on the hearth. "Be back in a minute." He went out the front door. When he returned, he had a hand grill with several fish fillets between it. Placing it above the hot coals, he spoke again. "Be ready in few minutes." He paused a moment. "Jim? Would ya mind gettin' the dishes from the cabinet?" He pointed at the one in the dining area, at the other end of the room.

I grabbed his glass of whisky and my gin and tonic and placed them on the dining table. Then went to the cabinet and pulled out some of the china pieces and held them up. "These?"

Daniel gave a quick glance. "Yeah."

I set the table with the plates and the flatware from the drawer in the cabinet. Then I carried the plates to Daniel.

He set them on the hearth. Taking off the lid of the iron pot, he spooned out some potatoes, using the large metal spoon hanging next to the fireplace. He put two fillets on my plate. "More?"

"Oh, that's fine."

He put the other four on his plate. "You take these to the table and I'll get the wine." This time, he took an oil lamp with him, as darkness had closed in on the cottage. When he got back, he went to the breakfront, got two wineglasses from the breakfront, and returned to the table. He poured wine into the glasses and handed me one. After he sat, he looked at me and raised his glass. "To a new friend." A big smile came to his face and he winked his left eye.

"To a new friend." I raised my glass.

The meal, though simple, was tasty. Conversation was light and we finished dinner rather fast.

Daniel started removing the dishes and wineglasses while I went in and sat at the piano. I took my drink with me. Since the music box had stopped, I set my drink down and began to play one of my favorite pieces, The Eighteenth Variation of Rachmaninoff's 'Rhapsody on a Theme of Paganini'. Surprisingly, the piano was in decent tune.

When I played the last note of the piece, Daniel spoke out. "It's a shame it's so short. Maybe you'll play it again? You were whistling it today when I bumped into you." He laughed.

I laughed, too. "You mean when the Klutz here, bumped into you . . . And I promise, I WILL get you another shirt. By the way, where is THAT shirt?"

"Got it hangin' up to dry. It'll make a nice keepsake to remember today." He picked up the bottle of wine and a lamp from the table, then started for the front door. "I'll put this away. We can have it with another meal, if you'd like to come to dinner again."

"Sounds good to me." I went over to fix another gin and tonic. "Want another drink?" I picked up his glass from the dining table and raised it in the air.

"Sure!" Daniel then went out.   When he returned, there were several chunks of ice in his hand. He dropped them in the two glasses.

Much of the conversation for the next few hours covered a multitude of subjects: from the beauty of the area, to the art of the old world masters, the architecture of the great cathedrals, and some light touch on our families and backgrounds.

Family matters seemed to strike a sensitive chord in Daniel, so I did not delve deeper, but my curiosity was sparked. Was there some deep dark secret in his past?

As time went on, I realized Daniel had not lit the light in the tower. "What about the light . . . in the tower?" I blurted out in the middle of our discussion.

"Oh! Not tonight. A ship's not due for a few days yet and there's no storm on the horizon."

"Sorry. I just thought. Oh, never mind. I don't know what I thought." I laughed and returned to the subject at hand. After a while, I thought about how late it was getting and how many drinks I'd consumed. Then I wondered how I was going to get back to the mainland.

Daniel must have seen the strange expression on my face. "Somethin' wrong?"

"I was just thinking about how I was going to get back."

Surprise and shock came to Daniel's face. "Oh God! I didn't think about that. I was so enjoying the time." He looked down at his glass of whisky then back at me. "Jim? I . . . Ah . . . Is it real important that you get back tonight? I mean, could you maybe spend the night? I'd sure hate to see us out there in the surf, with me in this condition."

I smiled thinking about it all. There was nothing pressing me the next day, and if it was all right with Daniel, it didn't matter to me. "Oh hell! Why not! Be the first time I've spent the night on an island. Much less one with a lighthouse."

"Great! You can sleep in my bed and I'll stay in my old room."

The matter addressed, we continued our conversation. Before we knew it, our talk became more personal. It was Daniel who addressed a subject of real personal meaning. But I don't think he meant for it to have the impact it did. He was hesitant in asking. "There's something I wanted to ask about your paintings. I noticed there are no people in them. Why's that?"

I was somewhat shocked by the question and tried to think of a good answer. Had he seen something I'd not thought of, something I'd not even asked myself? Was he being analytical or was it just an honest observation? To obscure my immediate feelings, I said something just to fill the silence. "Oh, I don't know. Just never wanted to put them in. People seem to get in the way." In my haste, had I spoken an inner secret truth? Had I given some clue to the real me?

His eyes stared deep into mine and seemed to look into my soul. The pause before he spoke was unsettling. "I thought they had a feeling of . . . well . . ." He paused again. "Your paintings are beautiful, don't get me wrong, but there's a sense of . . . loneliness." He continued to look at me.

What was I going to say? How was I to answer him? Without effort, he saw my inner self and I wasn't sure how to avoid answering, without telling a lie. Deep inside, I was a lonely person. All my life I'd sought love, but never could find it. Was it that obvious to someone I'd never met before? Was my life an open book?

I turned from his stare, still trying to think of something to say. The drinks I'd been consuming somehow allowed a crack in the protective wall around the secret, personal me. At that moment, it didn't seem to matter. The inner me began to spill out. In my fright of being exposed, I quickly spoke up. "I don't know how to answer that Daniel, without getting into a deep water. Maybe we can discuss this at some other time?" My efforts to patch the breech were successful.

"Sorry Jim. Didn't mean to pry. After all, it's none of my business. It's just that I know how it feels to be alone and lonely. Maybe we can talk about it sometime." He gave a sympathetic smile. "How about one more before we go to bed?"

I returned his smile. "Okay. One more."

We changed our discussion back to the architecture of the cathedrals of Europe as we finished our last drink. After a while longer, I glanced at the mantle clock. It was almost five o'clock in the morning.

"If you want, you can take a bath now. I'll heat some water." Daniel tried to be accommodating.

"Probably in the morning." I had taken a shower that afternoon.

"Here's a lamp. If you want, I'll show you to the bedroom."

"Oh, that's okay. I'm sure I'll have no problem." I took the lamp and headed for the stairs. On the first step, I turned to Daniel. "See you in the morning." I raised the lamp as a gesture of thanks and appreciation. I smiled.

Daniel's face reflected my own warm feelings. "In the morning." He winked his left eye.

As the amber glow filled the loft area, I could see a large double bed and matching antique mahogany furniture pieces. All were arranged in a cozy fashion in the angular space under the pitch of the roof. The handmade quilt on the bed was a work of art. I assumed Daniel's mother must have made it.

I undressed, blew out the lamp, then got into the cool bed. As my eyes adjusted to the dimness, I could see the glow from downstairs, coming up through the beams and reflecting off the slanted ceiling. I could barely hear Daniel shifting a few things around until the glow began to diminish. He was putting out the lights. Then there was the 'click' of a door handle. Momentarily, the last pale glimmer disappeared with the same 'click' sound.

The bed was comfortable, yet firm. As I began to relax, I became aware of the lulling sound of the surf breaking on the rocks somewhere out in the darkness. Before long, I was asleep.

CHAPTER IV

When my eyes opened, morning light filtered through the few windows of the cottage. The plucking tones of the music box lilted through the entire structure. The soothing melody was unfamiliar to me. "God, he's up already?"

Stretching and yawning, I gave a reluctant wiggle to getting out of bed. Then I smelled the coffee, chuckled, and yelled out loud. "I'll have a Spanish Omelet, toast, orange juice, and coffee! Maybe some strawberries and cream, too!" I continued to giggle as I got up and dressed. I caught a glimpse of myself in the mirror over the dresser. I ran my hand over my face. My five o'clock shadow was now at eleven o'clock. I ran my hand through my hair, trying to prevent it from looking like an explosion in a mattress factory.

When I reached the bottom of the stairs, I took a quick look out the window in the dining area. The sky was a clear cobalt blue. It was going to be another wonderful day.

Daniel was sitting on the hearth. The coffeepot was sitting near a small fire in the fireplace. Something was sizzling in the pan he was holding. He turned when he heard me. "Good morning." He winked his left eye. He poured coffee into one of the china cups sitting on the hearth, then some milk from a small container. He extended the cup in my direction. "Sorry. Don't have any strawberries, and I'm not sure how to fix a Spanish Omelet."

I took the cup and chuckled. "Just kidding. Thanks. Nothing like a good cup of coffee." I took a sip. It tasted great. "I'll have to show you how to make one of those omelets. You'll love it, I'm sure! It has all sorts of good things in it like onion, green pepper, celery, tomatoes, mushrooms, ham."

"Your eggs and ham will ready in a minute." He cracked several eggs into the pan. They bubbled and popped in the grease.

It was like smelling eggs and ham for the first time. There were two slices of bread standing in a holder facing the coals. Then I knew he was making toast.

At the same time, Daniel turned the metal contraption on its spindle so the other side of the bread would face the coals. Shortly, he was dishing out the eggs, ham and toast onto the plates.

I sat on the other side of the hearth and began to consume the tasty food. "Dan, this is terrific! There's something about cooking on an open fire. I almost have to laugh because I never eat breakfast."

"Glad you like it. If you want more, just let me know. We've got plenty."

When we finished eating, I indicated the need to get back and do a couple of things. He looked a bit sad that I had to go. "Do you think you might come back tonight? We've got to drink the wine real soon or it'll go bad. And I want to show you the light and all."

"How about I come back when I get finished today, and you can show me around." I was honest in my comment. I felt comfortable there and enjoyed Daniel's company. I wanted to come back more than he could know. Deep inside, I wanted to come back more than I knew.

Daniel was exuberant. "I like that idea! I'll watch for you on the shore and come for you in the skiff. I've got to polish the mirrors today and I can do that while you're gone. The barge is supposed to deliver the ice today for the cold storage cellar along with the week's food supply. We'll have plenty to eat."

"I want to do a painting of the lighthouse. Maybe I'll bring a canvas or two and my paints."

"Why don't you just come spend the time you need out here while you paint. I'd like the company, and to watch."

"I'd really like that Dan, and it sure would save me a lot of time going back and forth. I'll stop at the market and get a few things to help keep the food supply from getting low. Now it may take a little while to finish the painting, so if I get on your nerves, you have to promise you'll tell me to get back to the boarding house."

"I promise. And if I get on your nerves, you have to let me know, too."

As we stepped outside to walk to the skiff, the clean sea air hit my face. I stopped in my tracks and took a deep breath. The peace and calm that permeated the surroundings was intoxicating. I felt I was getting a new start, a new lease on time, a new beginning on life. Something inside me kept saying I was not going to regret this. I could also feel I was going to do something good with my painting. My heart was warm. I was content. I felt good about everything.

Daniel rowed the boat right to the shore. Even though the visor of the captain's hat shaded his face, I could see his eyes glint from the sunlight reflecting off the water. "I'll be watching for you."

I jumped out onto the sand and turned. Putting my hand up, I saluted. "Will see you when I get back, Captain!"

Daniel returned my smile and winked his left eye. "Okay matey! Give me a push off!"

"Aye! Aye! Captain!"

Daniel pulled on the oars. Within a few moments, he was out in the surf again, heading back to the island.

I watched for a few minutes, then gave a wave. I saw him give me a huge grin. That grin made me feel good. I was happy and full of the wonderful day.

It was interesting to me that the skiff looked so small out in the water. I mean, the wooden boat was some fifteen feet long with rather high sides and while sitting in it, there was some sense of security against the sea. But when viewed from afar, it looked quite small and no match for a major confrontation with very large waves.

I turned and ran to the car. Before I realized it, I was back at the boarding house. Gathering up my art supplies, a few changes of clothing, and my shaving equipment, I put them in the back seat of the car.

I stopped by the market and picked out some vegetables and meat. Since Daniel fixed dinner the night before, it was the least I could do to fix dinner tonight. I picked out some nice beef, and bought a bottle of decent red wine. I also bought several items I noticed were lacking in Daniel's kitchen, like plastic wrap, foil, a bottle of dish soap and plastic storage bags.

The gallery was my next stop, as I wanted to get some more information from Bob on the show in early September. There was another motive. I wanted to become friends with Bob. It never hurts to get in good with a gallery owner. After all, business is business. I was sure he would be very helpful.

I told him I'd bring a painting for him to see in about a week. It would still be wet, but he didn't mind, knowing it took some time for oils to dry. I already estimated it would take that long to complete the painting of the lighthouse island. Even without the first stroke on the canvas, he was anxious to see it. All artists need someone with that kind of enthusiasm. It's good for the ego.

He wanted to know if I had a frame yet for it, since he had an excellent selection. I was pleased with the samples he showed me and chose a six-inch wide framing of grayed weathered wood, with slight touches of black, pale blue and brown. The width of the frame and its colors would go well with the light gray stones of the light tower and cottage and enhance the ochers and blues of the sand, sea and sky. I also selected one for the painting I completed the day I met Daniel.

Once again in the car, I was on my way back to the light. It was early afternoon when I arrived and took three trips to get everything to the beach. Daniel saw me from the light chamber of the tower, when I was making the last trip.

Coming out onto the catwalk around the light chamber, he waved his arms over his head. I watched him disappear into the tower, finally emerging from the cottage door and down the stone steps. Before I could believe it, he was in the skiff and into the surf.

As I watched him rowing to the beach, a feeling of gladness came over me. I could not explain it. I knew I was going to have a wonderful time staying there. I felt all was well with the world, at least mine, and that God was smiling down on me for the first time in a long time.

Daniel rowed the bow of the boat right onto the sand. Within a moment, he jumped out and helped get everything into the skiff. I got in and sat in the back. He pushed the boat out into the water and we were off.

"Did the barge come?"

"Yep! Arrived right after you left."

Daniel looked like he had just swallowed the canary; he had such a big grin. Something was going on and I had no idea what it was. I assumed he was happy in anticipation of showing off his island. His strong arms pulled at the oars with the pace of urgency. He said nothing more.

When we arrived, we gathered up everything to go to the cottage. First, I took the food to the cold cellar. I discovered the location of the cellar the previous evening, nestled between the southern wall of the cottage and the curved northern wall of the light tower. While there, I opened the bottle of wine. It's always good to let a red wine breath at room temperature before it is enjoyed. Then I took the bottle of wine to the cottage and put it on the breakfront.

Looking up, I saw what Daniel was so anxious for me to see. He had hung the five paintings I brought the previous day. He stood there, wide-eyed, to see my reaction. His eyes sparkled like blue crystal, when he saw my reaction.

"Oh Dan, you didn't have to do that." The paintings looked as if they were meant to hang where he had placed them. My heart pounded as blood rushed through me. My emotions welled up inside me like a geyser. I had to fight to keep from crying.

"I hope you don't mind. They seem to belong here. We'll hang the seascape you finished yesterday, but you'll probably want to frame it first."

"It was real thoughtful of you to do this. Thanks for the compliment. You couldn't have done anything more to make me feel this good." His sensitivity and desire to make me feel at home touched a chord buried far within the walls of my being. I wanted to hug him, but I didn't. I just smiled. "They look real nice." I stood for some time seeing the change that had taken place in the room. A strange warmth came over me, like a part of me was being accepted into the house.

"Would you like to see the lighthouse now?" Daniel's voice broke my sensation.

"I'm ready. Let's go." As we started down the hall to the right of the fireplace, I quickly glanced back at the paintings. I was pleased how they fit into the house.

Daniel must have been reading my mind. "Thought since you were going to be here a while, we might as well enjoy them. I'll take them down when you leave." He was silent in a momentary secret thought. I wondered what it was because for a moment his expression went sad, then in an instant was happy again. "Now, let's go see my lighthouse."

At the end of the hall was the small door in the stone wall I had seen the night before. "This is the way to the light." When he operated the handle, I recognized the 'click' sound from the previous night.

We headed through the opening, into a dimly lighted stairwell.

The stone steps were about four feet wide, spiraling up and to the right. The outer wall of the tower was on the left and was periodically pierced with elongated peephole type windows. These were the only source of natural light.

"There are two landings and then the light platform. Between each are thirty steps. Come on, you'll see." Daniel started up then stopped on the third step. He reached into a small niche in the right wall and pulled out a small oil lamp. "I use this when it's dark in here." He replaced the lamp and continued up the stairs.

As we got closer to the first landing, the stairway became much brighter. The first landing was an open area with several small windows in the thick outer wall. The ceiling was domed to about twelve feet. The stone steps continued up on the outer wall, disappearing, as they spiraled upwards.

There was a pile of hay on the floor, a small table with a candle on it, a bench, a box of tools, a grinding wheel and several pieces of glass on the floor by the bench. On the hay were two blankets.

"Before Mom and Dad were gone, this used to be my room. I do my glasswork here now. Keeps from messing up the house."

I looked around the room. "I want to watch you some time. I want to see how you etch and make such intricate cuts in the glass." Daniel seemed pleased that I would want to know more about his hobby.

It didn't take an Einstein to realize this is where Daniel spent the last night. I was honored, but at the same time sad to find out that because of me, he gave up his bed and slept on the pile of hay. I asked him, point blank. "You slept here last night?"

"Sure, but I didn't mind." He was rather candid with me.

I felt rather embarrassed about the whole situation, but somehow I knew this problem would be corrected. "You're not spending another night here out of your bed. We'll talk about it later."

In the time I had talked with him, I came to the conclusion that Daniel could be nothing but honest. A lie was not in his nature. I don't think he knew how to lie.

Daniel looked around and grinned, as if telling some dark secret. "You know, I used to pretend this was a fort, and the windows were gun ports." He laughed, slightly embarrassed, at how childish his spontaneous confession must have sounded.

But who was I to judge? Who was I to throw stones? With some of the great *faux pas* I'd pulled in my life, I had no room to talk. I thought for a moment. "I think it's terrific. That was my first thought when I walked in. Guess I'll never grow up. And who cares!" I was honest. Maybe it was the 'Peter Pan' syndrome within me, but my first impression of the room was a fort, just as he saw it in his mind. I was glad I told Daniel, too.

From the expression on Daniel's face, I saw my confession had put him back at ease.

"Well let's get moving. There's sixty more steps to climb." He led the way up.

The second landing was much like the first, except smaller. This was logical, because as the tower got taller, it tapered. The only thing occupying this landing was a little table with a candle on it. There was a hole in the curved ceiling, near the stairs. A cable hung through the hole. On the cable were several iron weights. I would realize later, these were the weights of the works to turn the light mechanism.

We continued until we were within a few steps of the light chamber. I was now ahead of Daniel. He wanted me in front of him so I could see the view first, without him blocking it. But some six steps from the top, I froze. My hands pressed against the walls on either side. In my terror, I started to laugh.

"What's the matter?" Daniel bumped into me, I'd stopped so fast.

"Sorry Dan." I continued to laugh. "It's my acrophobia. I can't stand heights."

"Well wait, I'll help you." He grabbed my arms and was amazed at their rigidity. "You really are scared. What can I do?"

"Just let me relax a minute." I stood there a moment taking deep breaths. Daniel's reassuring manner helped me release some of the tension and I took a step. "That's some progress." I said as I laughed. It took a few minutes, but finally, with Daniel's help, I made it into the light chamber.

An almost delicate steel frame held the many glass panes, forming the circular outer wall of the light chamber. A paned door, on the west side, led to the catwalk around the outside. The chamber was not as horrifying as my mind had imagined, letting me relax that much further.

The view was spectacular. I could see for miles. It became quite evident, from this vantage point, the island was just off the southern tip of the rocky peninsula between the ocean and the inland waterway. Walking around the room to see in all directions, I noticed I could not see my car parked behind the near dunes. It didn't concern me. I knew it was all right.

"I should have brought my binoculars with me." I snapped my right fingers. "But I'll do it next time."

As I looked east, out to the open sea, Daniel began to talk in a low calm voice. "They use the channel as a place of refuge when there's a storm. The light's the reference to find the channel. Once they're in, they won't be crushed by the waves or be concerned about getting smashed on the rocks."

He paused for a moment, looking out across the ocean. "Been several times they didn't make it and ended up on the rocks or the beach."

There was a very long pause before he started again. The expression on his face changed to one of anguish and sadness. "It's like the night my Dad was comin' home. Mom and I were so anxious. We'd been watchin' a storm build in the distant east all afternoon. From up here I thought I could see Dad's ship many miles out. By early evening, the clouds were gray and angry looking, so I started the light burning. I ran down to tell Mom I thought I saw Dad's ship and it looked like he was trying to beat the storm. An hour later, the wind was at a gale and the waves were like mountains. I ran up here to see. The only light was this beam piercing the blackness and the flashes of lightning in the clouds."

"I could see the ship steering south for the channel. Then, it was being pushed toward the rocks. I couldn't understand why Dad hadn't taken all the factors into consideration. Something must have gone wrong. I found out later the mechanism to the rudder had snapped. There's nothing Dad could do. He'd lost all control of the ship.

The waves pushed it closer and closer to the rocks below. I ran out on the catwalk and yelled, but it was useless. Moments later, I heard the sound of the ship as it hit the rocks. In a death scream, it was being torn to pieces. I saw people jumping into the water trying to save themselves. Then I saw Dad, on what remained of the main deck. He was trying to help his passengers with their life preservers. It looked like he was telling them what to do once they were in the water. Then I saw Mom run out to the end of the island."

Daniel's eyes lowered, looking down at the eastern most point of the island. "She was waving as she ran. I yelled down, but she couldn't hear me, I guess. Dad must have seen her because he waved and looked right at her. By then, the ship was going under. Dad grabbed a piece of floating debris, as he slipped into the swirling water. The whole sight and sound was horrible: the screaming people in the water, the pounding waves on the dying ship, the cracking of the ship on the rocks."

I watched Daniel pause for some time, as if trying to gather an inner strength to finish telling of the event. I waited patiently, in silence. Finally, he started again.

"That's when I saw it, black and awesome. It was out there." He focused his eyes out toward the horizon, seeing something only visible in his mind. "It was like some huge moving wall, and I was helpless. That's what made it so terrible. I couldn't do a thing. My screams to Mom were lost in the wind. First, it hit the final remains of the ship, engulfing it and all in the water around it. Mom must have seen it then. I'd swear I heard her scream Dad's name as she stood fast. An instant later, the giant wave crashed against the point, sweeping her away, while it rushed on to the shore."

He paused again for a long moment. "They only found Dad's cap. Guess that's why I always wear it. How many of the people survived, no one knows. Just lucky, I guess. I was fourteen then."

"The town folk let me stay on as light keeper, and they pay me on a weekly basis. They buy my food and necessities out of the money and deliver them once a week. The rest of the money, they put in the bank for me. Some of the ladies give me a ham or a goose on special days, like Christmas. I'm real grateful for it.

I used to go into town when I was younger, but I got this funny feeling every time that they felt sorry for me and uncomfortable when I was around. So I stopped going. I don't mind. Least I don't feel funny anymore about the whole thing. I live in my world and they live in theirs. Guess it's better that way."

The whole time Daniel spoke, I felt I was watching a cup slowly pouring to empty. This was the untold story of his inner most pain. I knew in my heart, no one had heard it before, until now. But why me? What gave me the right to be the one? Could it be because I really listened to him? Because I actually gave a damn?

I began to think about his dilemma. No matter how you sliced it, he was a prisoner of the situation, with no way to escape. My life had been full compared to his. How horrible to be trapped, even in an Eden, and alone on top of it all. But why doesn't he just leave, move to the city, and become a computer expert? Then he could make lots of money, get married, have two point six kids, and be totally miserable. In time to come, we would discuss this further, now that he'd broken the ice. And because of our talks, he would come to heal in the knowledge he could have done nothing to save either of his parents. It was no one's fault.

I changed the subject for the moment. "Dan, show me how the light works. Then you must show me how the water works."

Daniel went through the total workings of the light. A crank, located in the light chamber would wind up the works, similar to that of a clock, and the light would turn for some twelve hours. The weights hanging in the second landing made the mechanism work.

When we reached the ground again, Daniel pointed out the oil storage tank. The oil was hand pumped from this tank, through a half-inch pipeline, to the smaller tank in the light chamber.

He also showed me the water collecting and storage system. The area formed by the surrounding stone walls of the cottage, the cold cellar and the tower was the large fresh water storage tank. The top of the tank was covered with wood. A spigot, located in the cellar, allowed the filling of a bucket or a large container. Location of the tank also protected it against the weather. Rainwater, running off the light tower, kept the tank full. This water was used for everything except drinking. The drinking water was delivered by the barge, in large glass bottles, and kept in the cold cellar.

It amazed me how virtually every drop that hit the tower was collected. Three gutter-like troughs were constructed in the stone around the tower, spaced evenly up the side. Rain hitting the walls of the tower would run down the face and into the gutters. From there, one down spout directed the water to the storage tank. Daniel said he'd never run out of water, even when he took a lot of baths, but he tried to be conservative.

There was a large stack of cut wood for the fireplace. It was delivered usually twice a year: once in the spring and once in the fall. This was paid for by the shipping companies, as was the oil for the light.

On the south side of the island was a very small area where there was one huge flat rock. Daniel indicated that at high tide it was only four feet above the surf. He liked to spend time there when he was swimming because it was secluded. The water was quite deep there, and since he liked to swim in the buff, the privacy was real nice, too. I laughed when he showed me the spot. I told him about an old swimming hole back home where we used to do the same thing.

"I'll have to see how deep the water really is there, one of these days." I laughed.

"Wait until you see how clear it is, too." Daniel added.

The only place he said we couldn't swim was where the sewage ran down and out into the water, on the northeastern side of the island. The stretch of the eastern point of the island made separation of the sewerage and the swimming rock a moot concern. I recognized the size of the ocean in relation to the amount of flow into it. It literally was the old expression of pissing in the ocean.

Since it was now late afternoon, I looked up at the sun and commented. "Think it's time for a gin and tonic."

"I could use a bit of a toddy myself." Daniel laughed. "You must show me how to fix your drink. It doesn't look that difficult to make."

"Okay! Lesson number one starts right now." We went inside.

I pulled the glasses out of the breakfront as Daniel went for ice from the cold cellar. I took out the decanter of gin, after Daniel returned, and poured about a half an inch into the glass. "That's how much gin I like in a glass this size." Then I reached for the tonic and unscrewed the top of the plastic bottle. I started pouring.

"Now that's something!" Daniel commented. "Flexible glass!"

"Well, you know, these plastic ones don't break in shipment." I was rather surprised at Daniel's comment, but passed it off as a product of being away from reality for so long. A truer thought could never have been more appropriate, at that moment.

I then cut one of the limes, squeezed it into the glass and stirred. "That's a gin and tonic!" I took a sip. "Ah! Great! Now, what are you having?"

Daniel grabbed his whisky and poured it over the ice in his glass. "That's all for me."

"Doesn't look like I'm going to get any painting done today." I walked over and sat down at the piano and started the 'Prelude in E Minor' by Chopin. When I finished, Daniel wanted me to continue. After two short Preludes, I looked up. "How about the music box?"

"You have to play one more piece first."

"Sure, if I know it."

"The one you played yesterday, the pretty one. You know."

I knew what he wanted and started the 'Eighteenth Variation' by Rachmaninoff.

Daniel was intent on hearing every note. He was like a sponge soaking up every drop of water it could. As the last 'D' chord faded, he sighed. "There's something haunting about that piece. But it's so beautiful." He placed his hand on my shoulder. "From now on, whenever I hear that melody, I'll think of you. Thanks, Jim." He went to the music box and cranked it.

My mind continued its many questions concerning Daniel and his life here on the island. It was obvious his knowledge was from the vast collection of books in the living room. But what held him here? Was he truly happy? I would let these and the other questions just be answered in time. "Okay! Since you fixed dinner last night, I'm fixing tonight. I want you to just sit back. If I need anything, I'll yell."

"That will be a change. You know, no one's ever made dinner for me since Mom."

"No one?" I turned in surprise. "Not anyone?" I could see the embarrassment in his eyes and on his face. All he had done was be sincere. But I couldn't let it rest. I had to open my big mouth again and put my foot in. I could not believe it. I made another stupid comment, causing pain. I pretended to make it appear it was a joke. "Well, just wait! . . . You're going to have a meal to remember. Just wait and see.”

Daniel dismissed my remarks. “What are we going to have?”

“Tonight we’re having fresh salad with my special vinegar and oil dressing, steamed broccoli, baked potatoes with butter and grilled steaks. How does that sound?”

“I can hardly wait. I’m starving.”

I checked the mantle clock. “How about dinner in one hour and twenty minutes?”

All Daniel did was smile.

“I’m going to need the sharpest knife you have and I’ll get started.” I headed for the kitchen.

“I’ll keep the fire going while you get things ready.” Daniel started out for more wood. “The knife’s in the drawer by the sink.”

I went out to the cold cellar for the meat and veggies. Returning to the kitchen, I washed off the potatoes and wrapped them in some of the aluminum foil I bought. I brought them to Daniel. “Put these in the hot coals and they’ll be ready by dinner.” I took the iron pot and placed it in the kitchen sink. I could not find a steaming colander anywhere in the kitchen, but that wasn’t a problem. When you cook, you learn how to improvise. "Dan, could you get me several small rocks from the beach? Make sure you wash them off, then half fill the pot with sea water."

While he was doing that, I prepped the salad things and put them in a plastic baggy. When Daniel returned, he took the bag to the cellar to keep it all cool. The broccoli would go into the iron pot when the water started to boil. Daniel placed the pot on the hanger in the fireplace. With the vinegar and oil I'd bought, along with some spicy brown mustard and other things, I made the salad dressing. I wanted the dressing to stay cool, so I put it in a small bowl, covered it with plastic wrap and put it in the cellar on one of the large blocks of ice. I chipped off several chunks for some drinks and returned to the cottage.

"How about another drink?" I knew he would answer in the affirmative and put ice in his glass.

"Okay." He turned to inquire. "Is there anything I can do?"

"Not a thing." I paused momentarily in making the drinks. "Now. How do you like your beef?"

"How do I like my beef?" Daniel reacted like I'd asked a question in some foreign language.

"Your steaks. How do you like your steak cooked?"

Daniel stared at me with a puzzled look. "Cooked, of course." Now knowing the reason why, I still smile when I recall that lost expression on his face.

I looked into the air with anguish. "Oh God! Another one who ruins his beef." Then I realized he probably knew nothing but well cooked meat, the island having no major refrigeration and the concern about the meat spoiling. "Okay! Experiment!" I watched Daniel. He seemed to be getting a kick out of this game. "I'm going to fix the meat my way first. And if you don't like it, we can put it back on the grill a little longer to cook more. How does that sound?"

"Why not! Gotta try new things once in a while." He bubbled with the excitement of trying something new.

I went into the kitchen to cut the meat into steaks. I would cook three of them. The rest I wrapped back in the butcher paper and ran them out to the cellar. I placed the package between two blocks of ice. Instant freezer, I laughed to myself.

When I returned, we sipped our drinks and waited for the potatoes to cook. Oh for my microwave oven!

To pass some time, I went and played the piano. Daniel enjoyed my playing. I found myself remembering pieces I hadn't played in years. This was nice since it kept the repertoire varied. Many of the hit songs form the 1940s, 50s and 60s, he'd never heard before. He liked virtually all of them, especially those with a melancholy theme. I realized that being out on the island with no radio or television did have some cultural drawbacks.

Before long, it was time to start everything. Daniel got his grill so I could put the steaks on the fire. I took the broccoli pieces and placed them on top of the rocks in the pot. This kept them out of the water so they could steam. I quickly put the lid back on the pot. I took the grill and held the steaks above the hot coals.

"Dan? Could you do me a favor? Get me the butter, salad stuff and the dressing. It's out in the cold cellar." There had been sufficient time for the open bottle of red wine on the breakfront to breathe. The table was set. Daniel did it while I had been playing the piano. All was ready and going well.

I pulled the potatoes out of the fire and set them aside. "Dan! The meat's almost ready! Bring the plates and I'll fix them. Put some butter on your broccoli and potatoes while they're hot."

Before we sat down, Daniel put a disk on the music box. He looked at me. "It smells so good." When he cut into his steak, a strange expression came to his eyes as he peered back at me. I could see he was trying hard to diplomatic, but couldn't find the right words. "Jim, it's not done." His voice was low and somber.

"It's done enough. Trust me. Just try it first. I told you, if you don't like it, we'll throw it back on the fire."

I watched Daniel slowly put the cut piece of meat in his mouth and chew. His eyes lighted and there was a smile as he swallowed. "It's so flavorful. Much better than before. But won't we get sick?"

"Have no fear. We won't get sick." I was pleased I hadn't lost another to the 'burn your meat' class.

Everything was eaten. There were no leftovers except for the half bottle of wine. I think if there had been more food, Daniel would have eaten it, too. The wine we'd save for another time.

He cleared the table and brought the dishes to the kitchen. As I lighted the lamps around the living room, I heard him call out. "I really like this new soap you brought in the flexible glass bottle. It's much nicer than the soap I've been using."

"Yeah. I noticed, last night, you didn't have any dish soap and picked some up today."

Daniel quickly finished the dishes and came into the living room. "Tonight, I light the light. They said a ship's coming in late. Was a bit unexpected, but you know how that goes." He headed for the tower.

"Mind if I come along?"

"I was sort of hoping you might sit up with me tonight, while I watch the light. We can sit in the second landing and talk."

"Oh sure. Why not. What's sleep anyway." I laughed.

Before long, the beam stretched out into the early evening dusk. Daniel wanted to go out on the catwalk because the heat was beginning to build up in the chamber room. The thought alone of going out there terrified the hell out of me.

"Dan, I can't. I just can't. I know the thing won't fall, but I just can't take the height." My body began to shiver with fear. "I'll lose my balance, I know I will."

"I promise I won't let you fall." He peered into my eyes. "I've got safety lines out there and I'll put one on you. If you get real scared, we'll come back in."

Daniel's eyes projected trust. How could I resist? I had to continue to try and overcome my fear. What better place than the top of a lighthouse to battle this affliction of the mind? Letting Daniel see this part of me, made me uneasy. It was my vulnerability showing. What would he think if I really freaked out? But he had been honest with me in his own flaws. I had to try. I was sure Daniel was sensitive enough to understand.

"Okay." I was reluctant.

Daniel led the way. Once I set the first foot on the walk, he had my arm. He tied a rope around my waist. It was attached to one of the steel rings on the framework of the wall. With a soft voice, he constantly reassured me.

I was surprised. The cool air and the sound of his voice were calming and I began to relax. His strong hand holding my arm was also helpful.

"Is it alright?" His genuine concern made me want to do better.

"So far so good." I laughed, trying to persuade my mind.

"We can go back." He gave me the option, if I was too afraid, without feeling conquered.

"No! No! I have to beat this thing somehow or another and I think this is helping." My body trembled like an earthquake.

"Well I think you're doing real well." Daniel was sympathetic, speaking like a doctor to his patient. "We'll just have to work on this, and in time, you'll come out here just like me."

The sun was well below the western horizon and darkness engulfed the day. I looked out to sea. Far out on the edge of the world, I caught a faint glint. "Is that a light?" I pointed and stepped forward, forgetting where I was. My body bolted in reaction to my instant slip of memory. I grabbed Daniel's arm like a vice.

"Don't worry." He spoke softly with assurance, then grabbed tighter on my arm to reinforce the knowledge that he was attentive. "Yeah. Does look like a light. Pretty far out, too. Be several hours before it gets here."

We stood on the catwalk for some time. It was a big help to my psyche to be there. The sound of the surf below and the cool salt sea air was very relaxing. Maybe I could beat this thing, I thought. Wouldn't that be an accomplishment?

After a while, I began to sense an inner desire. "How about some coffee? Think we're going to need some after staying up so late last night."

"Great idea." Daniel was having the same craving and helped me back into the light chamber.

I took the lamp and headed down the stairs to the cottage. After putting on the pot, I returned, bringing another lamp.

Daniel was up in the light chamber making sure all was well. I suggested we go back out on the catwalk, since there was a cool breeze out there. We'd be able to talk while we waited for the coffee. Needless to say, Daniel was quite surprised at my request.

"I'm not saying we have to hang off the railing." My sarcasm revealed the anxiety still inside me.

Daniel grinned, his eyes glinting in the amber light. "We'll have you cured before you know it. Just wait and see."

It took me a while to get out, but finally, I was sitting on the walk, leaning against the inner wall. Daniel started to sit across from me and lean against the railing. I thought my nerves were going into orbit, it scared me so badly.

"I know the railing's not going anywhere, but it just scares the hell out of me to think you might fall off." The whole thought of him falling from the tower was ingrained on my mind and there was nothing I could do about it.

Daniel repositioned himself next to me, looking out to sea. After a moment, he broke the silence. "Guess the coffee's about ready." He laughed, knowing how long it took me to get situated where I was.

"I'll be. I was so bent on getting out here, I forgot about the damn coffee. Son-of-a-bitch!" I started to get up.

"I'll go get it!" Daniel was quickly on his feet. "By the time you get up and into the light chamber, I'll be down and back again." He headed for the door. "Are you sure you're going to be alright?"

"Thanks Dan. I'll be just fine."

Daniel returned with a fully loaded tray. After pouring, he placed the pot near the heat of the light to keep it warm.

We sat for some time talking about things we both wanted to accomplish in the next few weeks. When I told Daniel I wanted to do his portrait and was planning to put it in the show, he felt a bit self-conscious. "But why not? You're a very handsome man. And that's an observance from an artist."

"But I've never thought I was . . ."

"Trust me! Truly handsome people never think of themselves that way. They are the ones who are not only handsome on the outside, but are handsome on the inside, too. Now I've only known you for two days, but I feel you definitely qualify for the "Handsome" category. Just wait until you see the finished product, then make your judgment. I already know it's going to be a terrific painting."

"Well." He was embarrassed. "If you say so." He hung his shaking head.

While sipping our coffee, we also covered the situation of the sleeping accommodations. I told Daniel it was ridiculous for him to sleep in the tower when it would be simple enough for me to sleep on the settee in the living room. If that wasn't suitable, we could sleep together in the bed in the loft. The bed was more than big enough.

"I think it's quite big enough, plenty of room." I continued.

"I just want to make sure you're comfortable." Daniel was being too considerate.

"Look! This is your house! You should not have to give up your bed for someone else. Now, I have no problem with the two of us sleeping in the same bed, if you don't. Listen! We're both adults, over twenty-one, so let's discuss this in an adult and logical manner. God! When I was growing up, I had to sleep with my brother because there weren't enough bedrooms for all of us. Nobody thought a thing about it! What really gets my ass is we get a little hair on our chests, doing the same thing, and people raise their eyebrows. They immediately think you're strange. I'm so sick of people's narrow-mindedness. Give me a break!" I paused for a minute to get off my high horse, then smiled. "So don't worry about me! I'll let you know if you're hogging the bed. Ever heard of an elbow to the ribs?" I started to laugh.

Daniel hung his head, slightly blushing, a big grin on his face. "Yeah. You're right. It's stupid to make an issue over something that's really quite simple. I have no problem with it at all. I just wasn't sure how you might react to the suggestion." He looked out to sea in a momentary reverie. "I can remember Mom joking about the elbow." He chuckled.

"Then it's settled?" I looked into Daniel's eyes.

Daniel smiled. "It's settled! And hey! Remind me never to get you mad at me. I'd like to keep my head."

We both sat laughing out loud.

CHAPTER V

I was at the cottage for nearly a week. The painting of the lighthouse island was turning out, beyond my expectations. I couldn't understand it. The images seemed to appear magically on the canvas, and so quickly. Never had a painting gone so well and with such inspiration. It was like I could do nothing wrong. Each brush stroke was perfect. The colors were vibrant and alive.

For some unknown reason, time was precious to me. I didn't want to waste a second. Maybe it was a fear of losing the touch. But there was more to it. Every waking moment was a pleasure. Never in my life had I been so happy and relaxed. Was I becoming too comfortable? Was there a reason why I was too happy? Was there some unknown force at work letting me paint better than ever, just to take it away, after a fleeting moment of brilliance? I was in awe of it all and yet terrified the bubble would burst in my face, when I least expected it. I wanted to get the portrait of Daniel completed before the magic disappeared. There was no doubt in my mind the portrait would be superb, but only if I didn't lose the feeling.

My time with Daniel was wonderful. We shared so many thoughts and viewpoints. His philosophies on life were a surprise, as they were like my own. Actually, they were VERY MUCH like my own. Our discussions, so far, made it obvious Daniel was not up on current events. But it didn't matter to me. They had no bearing on our existence on the island. The world could have blown up and it would have made no difference to me.

The island was a refuge unto itself. I was happy, enjoying life on this untouchable, remote world. I loved it. I appreciated the days so much more than when I was alone.

It was barge day, or I should say that's what we started calling the day the supply barge was to make its delivery. I got up early to work on the lighthouse painting. After a few hours, I readied myself to go into town. Gathering the wash, I was taking it with me because this, too, was laundry day. The simple life on the island made no great demands on our attire. What needed washing, fit in the small wicker basket I brought with me.

Before jumping out of the skiff, I told Daniel I would be gone a few hours. I took everything to the car while Daniel returned to the island to wait on the barge.

After completing the laundry, I stopped by the gallery to chat with Bob. I ordered a frame for the portrait I would soon start. It would be twenty-eight by thirty-six. I picked up some additional art supplies and canvases. Bob indicated I could pick up all the frames the next time I came in, since they would be ready in a few days.

I went by the boarding house to check the mail. I also picked up my camera and tripod. I wanted to take some pictures of Daniel and me. Next, I went by the market to get a few things I noticed we were running out of or hadn't acquired as yet.

Returning to my parking spot out at the dunes, I unloaded the car, taking everything to the beach. Daniel was coming out the door of the cold cellar when he saw me. He hurriedly went to the skiff to come pick me up.

When he arrived on the shore, I saw he was wearing the shirt with the paint spatters on it. As he jumped from the boat, I could see his whole personality was alive with gladness.

"What enticed you to wear that?" I chuckled.

"There was a man who takes pictures. He was with the folks on the barge and wanted to take a photograph of the lighthouse. He said the picture might be important in the future as a good example of older lighthouse structures. It would show the kind of work that existed when men took pride in what they built."

"But why the shirt?" Daniel had not answered my question yet.

"Well, let me finish. The man wanted me in the picture since I was the one who takes care of it. I put on this shirt because it just makes me think of a time when I first really smiled in a long time. And I wanted to smile for the picture. Just think! I might be put in a history book or something!"

"Well since you're dressed for it. I might as well take a few photos, too."

"You've got a camera?" Daniel seemed quite surprised.

I reached down, picking up the camera and tripod. "Sure." I set it up on the beach and readied it.

"Yours isn't as big as the one he had." Daniel examined the thirty-five millimeter cameras on the stand.

"His was probably a professional camera with better lens quality." I didn't really know the reason why, but I was ready to snap a few photos of Daniel. "Now, where were you standing?"

Daniel went to the spot. "Right here!"

"Okay. Now stand just like you did in the one for the man." I focused the lens and set the aperture while Daniel positioned himself with his legs apart, hands on hips and a big smile. "That's great! Hold it!"

The 'click' of the camera captured the moment forever on film.

"Now I'll get one of us both. Stay right there." I set the timer and pushed the button. Quickly, I ran and stood next to Daniel. "Get ready and smile."

With the next 'click', another photo was taken.

I snapped several more to finish out the roll of twenty-four pictures. I'd run them into town the next day and we'd have them in a week. Daniel was excited, knowing he would see them that soon.

With everything in the skiff, we were off to the island.

Life together on the island became routine with the things we did. Daniel always kept the fire going and I did the cooking. Daniel did the dishes, but we both helped with the housework. While I did the laundry and minor shopping, Daniel took care of the light. Several times I asked if he wanted to go into town with me, but he thought it best not to go. Just talking about it created anxiety for him.

I had no complaints. I was content. Thinking about it later, I would be amused how easily we adapted to and for one another. Life seemed perfect.

CHAPTER VI

I finally finished the painting of the island. So I was a week late. It didn't matter. Almost a month on the island had made me a new man. I was happy with life. It was the morning of barge day. The painting was finished just in time to take it with me to town. Signing my name, I was incredibly pleased with the completed work. It was like I was signing the painting of some great artist, but the work was really mine. My style was there, but more than that, the painting was alive. The scene was captured as I had never captured a scene before. It was light years better than the one I completed the day I met Daniel.

Daniel was very pleased, too. He was fond of the likeness of himself standing at the front door of the cottage. I think it gave him some sense of being part of something meaningful. He made one comment that made my heart warm. He said there was no loneliness in the painting.

Daniel looked at the painting, as I removed it from the easel. "I hate that you have to take it away."

"We'll get it back after the show. Don't worry."

"But what if someone buys it? How about I buy it first. Right now!"

"Dan, no, you won't buy it. I can't sell it to you."

Daniel looked very disappointed, wondering why he could not buy the work.

"I can't sell it to you, but I can give it to you."

Daniel's face blushed. "No! . . . No! . . . You can't do that. You can't make any money that way."

"It's okay. It means more to me for someone like you to have it than to sell it."

"Thanks Jim. What can I say." He winked his left eye and grinned.

When I arrived at the gallery, Bob brought out the frame I had ordered for the painting. Before I would let him see the painting, I put it in the frame. The frame was perfect. As I thought, the grays of the weathered wood, with touches of black and powder blue accenting the minor decorative bead work, complimented the stone of the light tower and cottage, the blues of the sky and sea, and the ochers of the sand. It set off the colors with simple elegance.

Bob almost jumped out of his skin. "It's truly unbelievable. I've seen seascapes and I've seen seascapes, but this one is more than

I could have dreamed of. I'm sure it'll have no problem placing in the show. I'm going to put it in one of the prime spots. I can hardly wait to see the other four you're going to put in the show."

"FOUR! . . . But I said a couple!" I almost lost my balance in surprise.

"Yeah! I know . . . But with work like yours, I was sort of hoping."

"Well, if I can complete that many between now and the show, and I feel good about them . . ."

"If they're anything like this, they're more than good enough." He paused looking at the canvas. "If you can get a few more like this in for the show, I know who'll be taking home all the ribbons. No one will be able to come close."

"Sure wish I could share your optimism." I laughed.

"Oh you damn artists! You never have faith in yourselves, especially ones like you . . . the good ones. Trust me! If you don't place, I'll eat the damn frame."

"I'll bring the salt and pepper." I joked.

Bob hung the painting on the wall at the front door. To do so, he removed another, already hanging there. Anyone coming in would have to be blind not to see it. He was candid with his comment. "I know you. I don't know this one."

He focused the spotlight directly at the canvas and stood back. "There! I swear, that has to be the best seascape I've ever seen. Real stroke of genius to put that man up there at the front door. Funny! . . . Looks like he belongs there. But I'm real surprised you left out the rose. You artists and your prerogatives. I know I'll never understand you."

I kept my mouth shut. There was no need saying something that could be construed as controversial. I was leaving at the end of the summer, but Daniel wasn't. A scandalous accusation, even if untrue, could make things intolerable for him and could possibly jeopardize a source of business for myself. My staying at the lighthouse was no one's business except Daniel's and mine. I wasn't sure what he meant about leaving out 'the rose', but I didn't ask.

"Well how much do you want me to put on it?"

I looked puzzled.

"The price! . . . How much? And don't sell yourself short."

"Ah . . . It's not for sale . . . I've already promised it to someone."

"Sure hope you got a good price. Now don't you sell anymore before the show. They'll be worth a lot more after it." Bob looked right at me. "Well, when can I expect the next one?"

I just laughed. "When I finish!" This must have been the feeling Michaelangelo had when being pressed by Pope Julius II to complete the ceiling of the Sistine Chapel.

I picked up the photographs from the drug store, stopped to check the mail at the boarding house, then headed back to the island.

When I told Daniel what happened at the gallery, he was ecstatic. "I knew everything would go well. And it's going to get better, just wait and see." His face beamed and he winked his left eye.

Then I showed Daniel the color snapshots. He was like a kid at the circus. He wanted to put the best one of us both on the mantle. I thought it was a fantastic idea. I also wanted the one of him standing in the pose requested by the professional photographer also on the mantle.

Since the light had to burn that night, Daniel had set up all my painting equipment on the second level of the tower, along with several lamps and candles. I joked that if Gainsborough could paint by candlelight, so could I. Daniel opened a few of the windows just enough to allow a gentle breeze to flow through the space. The portrait would be the subject matter for now. The canvas was large enough to do his face, virtually life-size.

Daniel sat for me until he went to check the light. While he did that, I went down and made some iced tea with lemon. I brought up the full pitcher and two glasses.

Daniel downed the first glass. "God! That's good!" He looked directly at me. "I don't know what I'm going to do when you go home. Probably starve to death. Best food I've ever had, since you started cooking."

"Thanks for the compliment. But I'm sure you'll do just fine. Someone who eats like you is never going to starve to death, believe me!" I started to laugh.

Daniel distorted his face to make it ugly, then started mocking me, shaking his head. "Someone who eats like you . . ." He joined the laughter.

By now, we were close enough and comfortable enough with each other, we could pick at one another and not think it serious sarcasm or criticism. We truly enjoyed each other's friendship and companionship.

Time passed quickly that night. Before I knew it, there was a glow in the eastern sky. The sun was coming up.

Suddenly, Daniel appeared from the chamber above. "Come on!" He grabbed my arm. "You have to see this from the point!"

We raced down the spiral stairs, carrying one of the lamps to light the way. Daniel set the lamp on the table in the living room as we passed through the cottage and out the door.

We ran around to the eastern side of the house and shortly, we stood in the cool breeze at the end of the eastern point of the island. Gradually, the water began to glow. The effect was so unusual. Soon, the orange ball of the sun slivered above the horizon. The transparent yellow beams streaked up and out to welcome the morning. We watched until the entire orb became yellow and was well above the surface.

"How gorgeous! Everyone should get up at least once in their life to see such an event. Dan, thanks for sharing this with me. I'll never forget it." We turned and walked back to the cottage.

Daniel went up and turned out the light. In the meantime, I turned off the lamps and blew out the candles on the second landing. Together, we extinguished the lamps in the cottage. It was bedtime. Within thirty minutes, all was calm, and we were in bed, asleep.

CHAPTER VII

Over the next several weeks, I worked not only on the portrait, but on two other canvases. One was a seascape and the other was a sailing ship. All had the lighthouse somewhere in the background.

Bob ordered frames for the other canvases and kept wanting to know when he could expect more of my work. He was pleased at the frame order. It gave him assurance I was doing additional paintings.

All was going incredibly well. After some lengthy conversation, Daniel convinced me to move into the cottage with him. Everything I had at the boarding house was stored on the second landing of the tower. The stereo, radio and TV were totally useless on the island, but having them there prevented the possibility of them being stolen from the boarding house.

To prevent anyone finding out about my living at the cottage, I went to town on the days the supply barge came. The time was planned to be away long enough for the barge to leave. Since my rooms at the boarding house had a private entrance, no one knew my comings and goings. Since I frequently picked up the mail, there was no evidence I wasn't staying there. I have to admit, there was something exhilarating about keeping it all very secretive.

During the time I was there, Daniel worked on several pieces of glass. They were turning out beautifully. I had no idea it took so much time to do even a small area. I finally convinced Daniel to let me show Bob some of his work, but I'd wait until after the show. Bob was so wrapped up with all the entries, I was afraid he would not devote the proper attention to appreciate Daniel's work. When Bob saw Daniel's glasswork, I was sure he would agree it was museum quality.

I had a chance to witness a major summer storm, while staying at the cottage. Daniel and I watched from the top of the tower. At first, I was afraid to go out on the catwalk, but with Daniel's help and reassuring confidence, I did it. The storm, although terrifying, had a strange beauty. The power of the mountainous waves was beyond description as they crashed onto the rocks. The wind blew like a hurricane. It lasted almost fifty-two hours, through which the light had to be kept burning. We shared the time caring for the light so neither of us would get tired.

CHAPTER VIII

As the summer rolled on, Daniel and I became closer. We were so accustomed to one another; we could almost anticipate each other's thoughts.

Many things I brought to the cottage, he first thought were strange, but he just accepted them, never questioning their existence.

I, too, had to get accustomed to different ways. The lack of electricity eliminated the possibility of having so many things I always took for granted. What made me glad was that none of it seemed to matter. There was much more to our lives than the conveniences of modern products and contraptions.

We were eating so well we started an evening exercise program to keep fit. I bought two inexpensive sets of three and five pound barbells for us to work with. When we finished, we would flip a coin to see who would take his bath first.

We shared our very beings with one another. We shared the colors of a sky at sunset as well as the magnificent wonder in the beauty of a seashell. Knowing there was someone else who appreciated what each of us was doing, seeing, or what ever, went beyond explanation. We went to the infinite with each other and yet, there was an infinity to go.

My life had meaning and purpose. I wasn't lonely anymore.

The ship painting and the seascape were completed simultaneously. Both were exceptional, even if I said so myself.

Bob was beside himself when he saw them. The area where he hung my work was the focal point of the gallery. He began to refer to it as the 'Jefferies Wing'. The last time I stopped by, he was overjoyed when I told him there would be one more, but it would not be finished for two more weeks. He didn't care. "I don't care if you're putting the finishing touches on it, two seconds before the judges walk in. Just get it here." He was adamant.

I would devote every spare moment to completing the portrait in time. I didn't tell Bob the subject matter, even though he tried to trick me several times to find out. Portraits were not in vogue, and I was afraid he might not want to consider it.

He was the only one who knew I was probably spending a lot of time out near the island. "You've really got this thing for that lighthouse. It shows up on all your canvases." He also knew I had a room at the boarding house, but had no idea I wasn't staying there.

I was living every minute to the fullest. Each day was a treasure to be savored. Every time a thought of going home came into my mind, I would repress it. Something deep inside me did not want to leave. Every time I thought of discussing my leaving with Daniel, I would choke up. A giant lump would form in my throat and stomach. The only way to stop from hurting was to think of something else.

Sometimes at night, I would lie staring into the darkness, thinking about the day I would have to go. A tear would run down into my ear. It just didn't seem fair to find happiness and then have to give it up, especially after such a short time.

I also wondered if my newfound creativity would disappear when I left. I just didn't want to think about it. But summer was drawing to a close and I had to address the subject with Daniel. I wondered what his reaction would be when I told him of the agony within my very soul.

Evenings, after dinner and Daniel finished the dishes, we would usually get a blanket, then go sit on the flat rock and talk. We would sip our drinks or a glass of my iced tea. Daniel had fallen in love with the iced tea I made. We never swam at night because Daniel said there could be sharks.

Sometimes we'd row to the shore and walk the beach while we talked. I loved it because there was never anyone to intrude. What amazed me was why no one ever discovered this beautiful area. But that was fine with me as I enjoyed the seclusion and peace.

I noticed one other thing, as the summer progressed. I was becoming more accomplished than I ever expected. There had not only been time to paint, but also to practice piano, do some creative cooking, help Daniel with the light, collect shells, walk, and talk. Everything was in earnest and with better quality than ever before in my life. I was sure it was my philosophy of being happy and relaxed that had a lot to do with it.

Even Bob commented on my state of mind. Jokingly, he asked me what drugs I was taking, because he thought they'd do wonders for him. He indicated I was much more alive and vibrant than when he first met me at summer's beginning.

I saw a big difference in Daniel, too. He had become much more outgoing. We were discussing it one evening and what he said probably summed it all up. He indicated it was all possible, because we were not alone anymore. We each broke from our shell of self and reached out for another. We knew we honestly and truthfully cared for another human being.

My mind went even further. Everything was so perfect. I always considered the closest thing to perfection to be love. Could it be that love had crept into my being without my even knowing it? Could it be I was in love? But in love with what? Was it the surroundings, the sea, the serenity, the simplicity? Or could it be something else, something I might not want to admit to myself?

CHAPTER IX

It was the beginning of September and the show was a week away. I was getting rather anxious about it. The results could be so important.

The portrait was finished and framed. But I found it hard to believe the painting was actually my work. It was impossible to think I'd ever be able to do another with such living qualities. I had captured the total essence of Daniel on the canvas. Daniel found it difficult to accept the fact that the man in the picture was really himself. It was his own modesty coming through again. Daniel was so confident about my work, he said he planned to go with me the day after the judging so he could see all the ribbons he knew I was going to win.

Before I showed the painting to Bob, I told him it was a portrait. I watched him cringe. But before he could say anything, I turned it around to his full view. His mouth fell open and there was a long pause before he spoke. "I would almost expect it to speak . . . and those eyes! I've never seen such eyes! It's like he's looking into my soul . . . Jim, this is the most inspired portrait I've ever seen. It's a masterpiece. It will be the hit of the show. Mark my words! A fitting centerpiece for the 'Jefferies Wing'. Now, don't tell me you sold this one, too?" One look in my eyes told him the answer. He was furious, but then smiled. He looked back at the canvas. "I'm sure he's the one who bought it, too . . . and deservedly so. Such a handsome devil."

I was fortunate Bob had taken such an interest in my work. The way he displayed the canvases made it impossible to miss seeing them. I was quite lucky.

CHAPTER X

The show was only a few days away, but I was totally relaxed. The pressure to finish the canvases was over. The only thing nagging at me now was the dreaded discussion with Daniel about me going home, after the show. It was inevitable, but I didn't know when it would happen.

It was early evening. Daniel and I sat quietly on the shore, looking out at the island. The setting sun made everything gleam as if it were sprinkled with gold dust.

Finally, I broke the silence. "Dan . . . When the show's over, I want you to have the portrait." I reached over giving a right jab to Daniel's left shoulder. "Maybe it'll be worth something some day." I chuckled, trying to give some humor to my voice.

Daniel sat silent for a moment, then quietly spoke. "Thanks, Jimmy." Then, without warning, he stood up and started running up the beach.

I watched for a split second, then realized something was amiss. What's going on? What's happening? I got up and yelled out. "Dan! Wait for me!" I started running after him.

Daniel was way out front, but finally stopped by a group of rocks. He turned, looking out to sea. Running as fast as I could, I was soon in voice range. I yelled again. "Dan! Hey Dan!" Walking up to him, I was almost out of breath.

He turned around. His large hands fidgeted with one another, fumbling in their nervousness. The fading light glinted off his wet cheeks. He'd been crying and his eyes were filled with tears. His mouth quivered and his whole body shook.

My whole being was pierced with extreme concern, seeing him like this. What was wrong? What was making him so upset?

He looked down for a moment at his fidgeting hands, then looked into my eyes. He began to cry as he spoke. "Jimmy? Why does everyone I care about, go away? Mom and Dad got taken from me and I had nobody. Now I care again . . . and you're gonna go away . . . I don't want you to go away!"

My heart shattered. It might as well have been a piece of Daniel's wonderful glass being thrown from the top of the tower to the rocks below. The subject I did not want to address and had repressed for so long was now coming down on me with the weight of the world. The harsh reality of it all was perfectly clear. I had only a few days left after the show, then I would be gone. Now, here was this hulk of a man, falling apart in front of me, his emotions pouring out. The pain of it flashed through my body as the pieces of my heart blew into oblivion.

At that instant, all my questions were answered. My friendship and caring had grown. I knew deep inside I did not want to leave him. HE was my inspiration. HE was the reason and the answer to all the 'whys'. My life was whole because of him. I could not settle for him being just a summer friend I saw three months out of the year. The strange had become real. I was in love with this man.

I leaned forward, hugging him tightly. "Dan? . . . I don't want to leave you either." I began to cry.

His arms hugged me. We stood there together, crying in our dilemma, saying nothing.

The sun went down and the air grew cool, but I was warm. We stood quietly together for some time until our tears were finally gone.

I began to think about my life, where I'd been and where I was going. Why should I cheat myself of this opportunity? What was so important that I had to leave someone who meant so much? There was not one good reason under the sun holding me in the city. I could rent out the house and put all my furniture in storage. As far as my waiter work was concerned, I could do it anywhere, even here. What other place could be more conducive to doing my painting? What more inspiration and encouragement did I need than Daniel's.

I looked up at Daniel. "I've thought about it all. We're going to work something out. Let's go talk about it."

Daniel perked up. A wide, warm grin filled his face. "Great idea! Let's go home."

We slowly walked back to the skiff.

I continued to think and weigh everything. I was too happy to let it slip through my fingers. I stopped short, turned and looked directly at Daniel. Even in the dim evening light I could see his face clearly. "Do you really think you could tolerate a permanent roommate?"

Daniel put both his hands on my shoulders, looking square into my eyes. "Are you serious? Do you really mean it? I can't believe you really mean it!"

I shook my head. "Yeah. I'm serious."

"Jimmy! You've made me so happy! It'll be wonderful! . . . You can paint and play the piano. I'll take care of the light and do my glass work . . . and . . . we won't be lonely, ever again." His blue eyes sparkled. He picked me up and danced me around, like a child with a rag doll. "You won't be sorry. I promise." He set me down and ran out to where the waves meet the sand. He tilted his head back, looking up into the sky, then cupped his hands around his mouth. "Thank you, God!" He yelled. "Thanks for sending me a friend . . . someone to love. I promise I'll be good to him." He turned, looking at me, his face beaming.

My own gladness grabbed me. I, too, ran to the water, tilting my head back. "Thank you, God, for letting me find a friend. I promise I'll be good to him, too."

We began to laugh and slap each other on the back.

As we walked to the skiff, I began to think of the future and how good it was going to be. There was so much we could offer one another. I also thought of how fond I'd become of Daniel. His companionship and easygoing ways were so comforting to share. Maybe I did care too much, but it didn't matter to me. I knew, deep in my heart, I was content in my feelings.

When we reached the island, Daniel jumped out, pulling the skiff to the mooring post. I ran across the sand toward the steps up to the cottage. "Last one up's a rotten egg!" I laughed and started up.

"Oh yeah?" Daniel was right behind me.

Half way to the top, I felt my body being lifted and seemingly fly through the air.

"Now! . . . Who's the rotten egg?" Daniel laughed, setting me back on the ground.

"Not fair! Not fair!" I protested.

Opening the front door, Daniel stopped and turned to look at me. "Jimmy, you've always belonged here. I knew it the first day you walked in."

"That was a nice thing to say." I was surprised to hear him say something I'd felt from the very first day myself. I knew I belonged there, too. It was inexplicable. "Dan . . . You've made me feel so comfortable and at home. You're the one who made me feel I belonged here."

We walked in and I went to the breakfront to make us a drink. Daniel went to the cold cellar to get some ice. Soon we sat down to talk.

Daniel smiled and winked his left eye. "Well, it's OUR house now. And you know? It feels good to say it. Jimmy, I've always been so lonely since Mom and Dad. But I never knew how lonely, until there was you. And the thought of you leaving was about to break my heart." He paused for a few seconds. "I realize it's a little unusual for a man to care so much for another man. But I've done a lot of thinking about it all. I believe if it weren't meant to be, God would never have let it happen. I was alone in this world and needed someone to love. You know, I've never loved anybody since Mom and Dad. But this! This is different. I don't know how to explain it." He stopped for a moment. "And I've never said it to anybody either." He paused again for a moment. Then without hesitation or self-questioning, he looked into my eyes. "Jimmy. I love you, Jimmy. You make me alive. Please don't ever go away from me."

I had never allowed myself the luxury of a relationship with anyone. No one had ever touched the inner me. Now I was being bowled over by sincerity and assuredness. He'd made me have feelings I'd never had before. His words touched my heart making me accept the fact that what I felt toward him was much more than just friendship. Although I smiled, a tear ran down my face. "Dan. I love you, too, more than you'll ever know."

We stood and gave each other a big hug.

For the first time in my adult life, I felt safe, secure in the knowledge I was truly loved. Regardless of how difficult the problems, I would fight, if necessary, to keep what we had from being taken away. I could be starving, but I'd be alive in the fact I was loved by Daniel. My life, in the past, had only been existing. My life, now, would be living.

During and after dinner, we discussed all the things we wanted to do. We started making plans that would take us a hundred years to complete. Daniel suggested I bring all my things from where I lived in the city and store them on the landings of the light tower, instead of putting them in storage. This seemed logical and would save the storage fees.

I was excited about this major step in my life, the adventure of it, yet softened by the simplicity of it all. I could feel in my heart my life was going to be better than it had ever been before. I was truly happy.

CHAPTER XI

The next day, I went into town to do a few errands. The first stop was the gallery. I wanted to see the other entries in the show. Bob had everything set up. The show would begin in two days. The judging would take place on the third day.

All the entries were superb. It was obvious the competition would be fierce. The way Bob had my work displayed was beyond expectation. The portrait of Daniel, standing at the ship's wheel, his blue eyes peering out, was in the most advantageous place. It seemed to be the center of the collection. All four paintings had pin lights on them, making the paints seem to come alive.

"Well, what do you think?" Bob questioned his positioning of the works.

"I think everything looks just great, especially the way you've made my work look like the center of the show. No one could miss seeing them. I swear the other artists will think there's payola going on here."

"That was part of the object. Good work should have its recognition. And speaking of payola, I really want to talk to you about keeping some of your work here after you leave for home."

"Well . . . What if I told you I'd like to discuss the possibilities of you representing my work, because I've decided to move to the area?"

"You're kidding! A dream come true! There is a God!" Bob

waved his hands in the air. "No need to ask twice! Consider it done!"

"There's someone else's work I'd like you to see. I think you might like to represent him, too. Thought I'd bring you some of his pieces after the show."

"Great! If it's anything of the quality of your work, I'd love to see it. But do wait until after the zoo parade of this show. It's about to kill me."

I turned to leave, then yelled back. "Wish me luck in the show."

"Luck? . . . You don't need it! I know who's going to run away with all the ribbons. I feel sorry for the other poor slobs that have to compete with you." He laughed.

There were just a few pieces of mail at the boarding house, most of it to the mysterious person called 'Occupant'. One was for the other notorious person named 'Resident'.

Before disconnecting my phone, I called the landlady to thank her for the wonderful accommodations that summer. She expressed hopes I'd come back the next year. I put the phone in the car. It would be placed with my TV, stereo, radio, LPs, and other things I'd already moved out to the island, which were now stored on the landings of the light tower.

If I was going to live out there, I was determined we'd get some sort of power, even if it meant getting a small generator. Of course it would be put in an inconspicuous place. Nothing was going to destroy the beauty of the island. But if it came right down to it, I'd do without, just to preserve the serenity. I could think of nothing more ugly than those stupid electric and phone lines strung all over God's creation, bastardizing the view. Maybe we could have them run under ground, or under water in this case.

The dinner I planned that night was going to be wonderful. My special Seafood Alfredo was too good to be true, even if I said so myself. I picked up all the items at the grocery store.

While walking to the car, I passed the little hardware store that was next to the market. My eye caught a glimpse of something yellow, in the garden section. Putting the groceries in the car, I went to investigate.

It was a single rose on a small bush, packaged as a sale item. I could not recall ever seeing such a rose. The petals were a bright shade of yellow, edged slightly with a touch of pink. Although somewhat like a 'Peace' rose, the pink was not as pronounced. I took one sniff of the flower. The fragrance was intoxicating. Not only was it beautiful, but it smelled good, too. I loved it.

The salesman indicated it was the last rose bush they had, it being a leftover from the spring shipment. The time of the year was wrong to be selling them. He said it was a rambler, but the nametag got lost and this was the first time it ever bloomed. "I'll sell it to you for fifty cents. Just to get rid of it. But I can't promise it will live."

"I'll take real good care of it. Who knows? It might outlive us all." I laughed.

It was for Daniel. And who could say? Maybe the rose would live. I also bought some bone meal and rose fertilizer. "Could you put it all in a large bag and staple it closed?" I asked the salesman. "It's for a friend and I want it to be a surprise."

While driving out, I thought how strange it felt to say 'home' and refer to a lighthouse on an island. But it was more than a tower of stone and a slate roofed cottage. It was also the wonderful, caring heart waiting there for me. I was warm at the thought.

I grabbed everything, after parking the car, and carried it to the beach. Looking out across the water, I saw Daniel waiting at the front door. He waved and headed for the skiff.

When he landed, he was all smiles, like he had some neat secret. It reminded me of the day he came to get me when he'd hung the paintings on the walls.

I looked directly at him. "Okay! What's up?"

Daniel's eyes sparkled and his grin went from ear to ear. "What? What do you mean?"

I didn't want to ruin the surprise, so I just didn't press the issue. As a matter of fact, I completely changed the subject. "We're going to have a terrific meal tonight. Think you're really going to like it. I also bought something else." I picked up the bag containing the rose bush and fertilizer. "It's for you, but it's for the house. You'll understand when you see it. I'll let you open it later."

We put everything in the skiff and were off. Daniel pulled furiously at the oars the same as that day. There was something going on at the house. He really wanted to get back in a hurry. Of course, my curiosity was running wild, but I stayed calm.

When the boat landed, Daniel swept everything up in his great hands. Within seconds, we headed for the steps.

Reaching the cottage, I opened the door and walked in. The room was softly lit with candles and lamps, even though it was just late afternoon outside. Daniel quickly put the bags of groceries in the kitchen and returned to my side. I waited patiently, knowing he wanted to see my reaction to the special secret. I set the bag, containing the rose bush, down on the floor, next to the door. "This is for later."

I walked further, until I could see the dining area. The chandelier was aglow. In the middle of the table was a vase of beautiful flowers he'd picked from around the rocks on the island. The table was completely set with the china and flatware. Then I saw the glasses. I slowly walked over, Daniel right behind. It was clear.

Each place setting had one entire set of glasses from the breakfront. All those at Daniel's place had his name engraved on them, surrounded with the intricate vines and leaves. Those at my place had the same design of vines and leaves, except they surrounded my name.

I picked up one of the goblets from my place, slowly running my finger over the delicate work. My heart was filled with emotion. "Oh Dan." I started to cry. "All the work . . . They're so beautiful." I turned looking up into his beaming face.

"You really like them?" His voice was soft and calm.

"Like them?" I wiped the tears from my eyes. "They're absolutely stunning."

He smiled warmly. "To you . . . with all my love."

I gave him a big hug. "Thank you. More than you'll ever know."

I examined the others at my place. The work was truly elegant. I picked up the goblet again and walked over to Daniel's place, picking up the matching glass. I placed them side by side, holding them up to the light. "Just think! One of the long, lost, unborn relatives will inherit these some day. I wonder if they'll truly understand? I doubt it. To them, they'll just be two names on some old glasses . . . and who knows? There might even be some outrageously lurid and scandalous tale to go with them." I chuckled. "It's such a shame they'll never know the love that's here. But that's okay . . . We know . . . And that's all that matters."

I set the glasses gently down then turned to Daniel. "Thank you so much for everything . . . and for you." I paused. "I love you, Daniel Coffin." I hugged him again.

I picked the glass up once more. "But how? When did you find the time?"

"Oh . . . When you were painting, and sometimes when you were in town, and once in a while when you were asleep. When you really want to do something, you find the time." Daniel gave a sly look. "That's not all . . . But that will have to wait until after dinner."

"There's more?" I questioned.

"One little thing more . . . But that will wait. It has to be dark to appreciate it."

"Now for you." I ran back to the front door and picked up the bag. "Just a little something to say I was thinking about you." I handed Daniel the bag.

He was like a child opening a fragile but special present. When he saw what it was, he reacted as if it were gold. "Oh Jimmy. It is so beautiful. We can plant it next to the front door. On the right, so we can see it every time we come in." He held the single blossom to his nose. He sighed. "And it smells so nice."

At dinner, we toasted our friendship with the beautiful glasses. Daniel really pigged out on the Alfredo.

"You're going to look like a whale if you keep eating like this." I joked.

Daniel just grinned, winked his left eye, and finished his third helping. He was obviously satisfied with the dish.

With dinner over, Daniel cleared the table and did the dishes, except for the wine goblets. Afterwards, he grabbed my arm with one hand and the wine bottle with the other. "Now! . . . The last thing." I picked up the goblets on the way to the door to the tower.

Daniel lit the lamp at the third step and we headed to the top of the tower. When we reached the light chamber, he positioned the lamp on a little table he'd set by the east wall. "Okay! To see this, we need to go out on the catwalk."

Through the summer, I worked on my phobia, making some headway. But it was still there, lurking in my mind.

He opened the door and we stepped out to a cool breeze. It felt refreshing on my face. Daniel guided me around to the east side.

Finally, I saw it. The glow of the lamp inside and behind it made it clearly visible. The amber light accented the heavily ornamented twelve-inch square pane. The elaborate cut and etch work intertwined around the central area where there were four initials, interlaced to form an incredible monogram. I could make out the two "J"s, the "D" and the "C". It was a splendid work of art. Among the vines of leaves and flowers, and around the monogram, were the words "I LOVE YOU, JIM . . . DAN".

"What can I say? It's so beautiful, and the words are so . . .." I started to cry again. "Why did it take so long for us? It doesn't seem fair we had to wait so long."

Daniel was behind me. He put both his arms around me. "I changed the pane out today. Now, when the light's burning, it'll shine love out across the endless ocean. It'll go on forever."

I thought about what he just said. "It'll shine on as long as there's a lighthouse. It'll probably be here when we're dead and gone. I think that's what's so terrific, too. Through your glass work and my painting, our love will outlive us both."

"Well, I wanted to do something special for you, and I was so afraid you might leave before I got it all done. I wanted you to see how much I cared for you. Maybe me finishing it all helped God to realize I didn't want you to go."

I turned, looking up at him. "Dan, that's such a nice thing to say." I looked back at the pane. "Bob is going to flip when he sees your work. We'll give him so much to put in the gallery, he'll have to build another wing or get a larger gallery. And we're going to make a ton of money. Then we'll go to Europe and I can show you all the great buildings, cathedrals, museums and sights over there. I can't wait."

"Sounds great to me. Can't think of anyone I'd rather go with."

"And I can teach you to paint. We'll both have paintings in the gallery. How do you like them apples?"

"You really think you can teach me to paint? You have to be kidding?"

"Technique! Technique! I can teach you technique. You'll have your own style. That's what's important, so it doesn't matter. And you'll be great! With your sensitivity, sense of balance and composition, and innate abilities, it'll be a snap."

We talked long into the night of the many possibilities that lay in front of us. Instead of the hundred years, it was going to take us three hundred years to do everything. Life was going to be so wonderful for us both.

CHAPTER XII

We got up early the next morning because Daniel wanted to plant the rose bush. He dug a hole to the right of the front door.

"Jimmy, if you'll get some water, we'll be ready to plant our rose bush. I've mixed some of the bone meal and fertilizer with the dirt."

"I think it'll really be pretty when it grows up over the door and along the roof." I paused for a moment. "But you know, the guy at the store said it might not live."

Daniel looked up at me. "If I have anything to say about it, it will last forever. Mark my words." He patted the bush.

I smiled at Daniel. "I'll remember that." I started to laugh.

Daniel shook his head. Still kneeling on the ground, he looked up to the sky. "God! Help me watch over this rose bush to show that I love and care for my friend." He then turned and peered into my eyes. A serious cast came to his face. "My love for you WILL keep the rose alive." He stood up and gave me a big hug.

After a good watering, we stood back and looked at the bush. Then we looked at one another.

"It will be real pretty, I know." Daniel looked up and over the door, like he was seeing the bush in its mature state, growing up and over, hanging with hundreds of blossoms.

Daniel wanted to rest, because he had to watch the light that night. A ship was coming in. I would help, since I'd become well versed with its workings.

I did some cooking while he slept. I started the spaghetti sauce as soon as Daniel went to lie down.

A little after noon, Daniel appeared at the kitchen door, standing in his white under shorts and cap. "I could smell it cooking while I was sleeping. It smells so good, I just couldn't resist coming down to tell you." His face was aglow and happy. His eyes glinted as he winked the left one.

"You should be resting." I laughed, holding out a spoon of the sauce. "But since you're up. Here! . . . Taste this and see what you think."

"Great! When can I have some?"

"There are no noodles yet."

"How about on some bread?"

"I swear! You're going to look like an elephant." I shook my head and reached for a plate. There was no way to resist his charm.

He sat and began to eat the little snack I'd fixed for him. "You've got to be the best cook in the world." He looked up into the air. "Sorry Mom! But if you could taste his cooking, you'd agree." He looked back at me. "You know we'll never get fat. It's not in our nature. We're too active. And anyway, it'll put hair on your chest."

I laughed. "You haven't got another square inch left for it to grow. There's no more room."

Daniel laughed as he looked down at his chest. "Well. Maybe it'll get thicker."

"You're absolutely incorrigible!" I shook my head.

Daniel finished his plate then returned to the loft to rest some more. I divided the sauce into plastic bags and put them into the cold cellar between the blocks of ice. After cleaning the kitchen, I checked the dough I was prepping to make bread.

Raised yeast bread is one of those things that takes forever to make. For me, I was never successful in making it. The first time I tried, when I was ten, the loaf was like a lead sinker. I could never get the dough to turn out right. After several tries, I gave up. Raised bread was something I could not do. But here I was, making yeast bread, and by God, it was turning out just fine. I couldn't believe it. Another thing amazed me. I was actually taking the time to do this laborious and tedious task, and enjoying it. Maybe I had some screw loose? I laughed to myself.

As the afternoon sun lowered, Daniel came down again, still in his under shorts. "Looked out the window. The wind's picking up. We might get a storm tonight." He took off his hat, scratched his head as he yawned, then put the hat back on.

"Is everything ready for the light?" I began to place the loaves into the oven.

"Yeah. Think I'll get up there and get it all started."

"Okay. I'll bring you a cup of coffee in a few minutes. It's almost done. We can watch the sunset together."

By the time I reached the top of the tower, the light was burning brightly. I set the tray, containing the pot and cups, on the small table. Quickly, I glanced at the pane in the east wall. It sparkled in the brilliance of the light.

Daniel took a sip. "Tastes good. Thanks." He stood there looking east. The reflected light, off the windowpanes, glinted in his eyes. The golden glow made his tanned body a soft bronze color, his white under shorts an ivory and his hair a warm soot. "Let's go watch the sun go down." He headed for the door.

We sat with our backs against the west wall, our legs stretched out over the catwalk. The breeze seemed cooler than normal. We watched until the last rays vanished and the blanket of darkness covered the sky.

Daniel put his right arm over my shoulders. "You know, I've been thinking about what you said, about why it took so long for us to meet. And you're right. It doesn't seem fair we had to wait so long."

"I know. Seems we wasted so much time. Time we can't get back. But I guess it's like all things. Nothing is to happen until it's time for it to happen. Everything in its own time. If we'd met sooner, maybe we wouldn't have been ready for a friendship such as ours. I try not to think about all the time that's gone by or all the water that's gone under the bridge. I'm thinking about the future. OUR future. We've got all that in front of us, and for that I'm grateful."

"I guess. But I sure wish we could have met sooner. I wouldn't have been lonely so long."

"Well are you hungry? I'm going down and fix dinner real quick. Won't take too long. The bread should be just about done."

"Need any help?"

"No. Just keep the light going. I'll be back before you know it."

And so it was. I took the bread from the oven with great glee. It had turned out perfectly. In no time at all, I fixed two plates of spaghetti, with some of the hot, fresh bread, and was bringing them back up to the top of the tower.

We sat in the light chamber while we ate. Afterwards, we poured another cup of coffee and went back out on the catwalk.

Looking out, we could see no sign of a ship, but there were distant flashes in the eastern sky. Daniel was sure there would be a storm. The waves got rougher. They crashed on the rocks below with such force, the sound was frightening.

The scene made me shiver. A subtle chill raced through my body. "Someone walked on my grave." I spoke softly.

"What? I didn't hear you."

"Oh, nothing. Just a little chill."

Daniel stood behind, wrapping his arms around me. "Don't want you to get sick."

I continued to look out into the darkness. The cool wet wind chilled my face. Something foreboding and sinister crept into my mind. I spoke slowly and calmly. "Dan? If something was to happen, would you remember me?"

"What? What do you mean? Is something wrong? Are you alright?" His arms gripped me tighter. "You didn't change your mind? You're not going to leave? Oh, Jimmy. Please don't leave me. I don't know what I'd do if you left."

I turned, hugging him. "No. I'd never leave. Not intentionally. But if something did happen, I want you to remember the good times. We've had some real good times."

"Jim. Don't do this. It's scary."

I looked up into Daniel's face. "It's just that I'm so afraid the bubble will break. And I know so well we only have this one chance, at least in this life. There are no second chances. We have to live for now. No one's guaranteed tomorrow."

Daniel's eyes glinted and he smiled. "You've given me the best times I've ever had in this life. To lose you would break my heart. But I'd remember you until the day I died."

We stood there for some time, saying nothing more.

Suddenly, a bright flash of lightning appeared many miles out to sea. Several seconds later, the low rumbling built to a small crescendo, then diminished away.

I looked up at Daniel. "How about some more coffee?"

Daniel looked down with a big smile. He winked his left eye. "God would never let anything happen to you, to take you away from me."

I laughed. "I promise! I promise I'll never leave. And if I do, you're coming with me. You took too long to find. You don't think I'm going to let the best thing that's ever happened to me in my life slip away? Not by a long shot!" I stood back and softly hit him in the stomach with my fist. "Now! What do you think about that?"

Daniel grinned and winked his left eye again. "Let's have some more coffee."

Finally, the late night storm reached the lighthouse and we had to go inside. It rained and the wind blew, but the waves seemed out of synch with the storm. They belonged to some raging invisible hurricane.

Because the air was rather cool, we both went and put on warmer clothing. We sat watching all night. I went down, every once in a while, to get us both a snack and more coffee. I also made a pitcher of iced tea with lemon, Daniel liked so well.

The storm continued, while the hours passed. It was around six-thirty in the morning when we heard it. The sound of a distant horn. "That's it!" Daniel strained to see out into the early dawn. "Let's go out on the walk. We might be able to see it that way."

As we went out the door, Daniel tied a safety line around me in case of some unforeseen accident. He looked at me, the raindrops running down his face. He grinned and winked his left eye. "I'm not going to lose you that easily."

Coming around to the eastern side of the light, I cupped my hands around my eyes to block the brightness of the light. To the southeast, I thought I saw a dim point. It was in the same direction as the horn sound. "Is that it, Dan?" I pointed.

He looked in the direction I indicated. "That's it! She'll be reaching the inlet in an hour."

I continued to watch as the vessel came closer. The coming dawn and the flashes of lightning finally made it quite clear. It was a vintage, three-masted clipper.

My eyes opened wide, thinking they had deceived me. But the next flash of lightning reassured me, they were correct. It was a real treat to see a late nineteenth century wooden sailing ship, as there weren't many of them left now. I couldn't understand why anyone would put one of those beautiful old vessels in peril, if a storm was expected. Most of the sails had been lowered on the three tall masts. Those still unfurled were beginning to split and shred from the merciless wind. Crewmen were scampering all over the ship and its riggings, seemingly to make sure all was being done to prevent disaster. But the ship was tossed about like an aimless cork in the waves.

"Damn! Something's wrong!" Daniel pounded the railing. "She's not compensating for the current. Steer south!" He yelled. "If she doesn't turn south, she's going to hit the damn rocks for sure!"

I watched, twisting my body, thinking my gyrations would somehow help move the ship out of harm's way. There had to be some problem on board. No one in their right mind would just let a ship like that run aground.

The wind and waves carried the vessel more and more to the northwest, toward the lighthouse and the rocks. Suddenly, the ship began to turn.

"It's turning! The ship's turning!" I jumped up and down with joy.

Daniel stood silent, watching the drama unfold in front of us. "It'll be a miracle if she makes it!"

Slowly, the graceful clipper moved to the south. The wind lashed through her rigging and a few shredded sails. Waves crashed against her sides, sending spray and foam onto the decks. There were a few flashes in the sky, lighting the whole scene. The entire panorama looked so unreal, it reminded me of a bizarre stage set.

Suddenly, a great huge wave lifted the ship high into the air. When it receded, there was an excruciating sound of splintering and snapping timbers. It was a death scream. The ship was on the large group of rocks, just south of the island. The sound of wet wood against stone was accompanied by a loud crack. The front mast fell across the bow. Instantly, the decks were alive with passengers and crew.

The scene was tragic. I had feelings for the safety of those on board, but I also felt an enormous loss for another wonderful example of the great sailing ships, the likes of which will never be seen again. A part of history was slowly being taken from us. My whole being ripped as I watched in horror of it all.

"Jimmy. I have to go help." Daniel spoke soberly and headed for the door.

Daniel's voice snapped me back to my senses again. "Wait for me! Four hands are better than two! You can manage the oars and I can pull them out of the water!" I was right behind Daniel.

Within minutes, we were in the skiff, rounding the western side of the island and heading toward the ship. Daniel maneuvered the small boat through the rocks and waves until we were almost at the ship's side. Several people were already in the water. Retrieving them, we headed for the island, as it was the closest drop point.

Returning, I could see several people at the edge of the decks, yelling for us to come. Some of the crew were lowering the two on-board lifeboats filled with passengers. Others helped to lower women and children into our skiff. This is when I noticed they were all wearing period costumes. I quickly dismissed it, thinking there had been a festival somewhere.

The rescue effort was going well and without panic. All were being ferried to the island. In no time at all, nearly everyone was safely on the island. Daniel and I headed out for the last few. The other boats were right behind.

By now, the decks were in the water, the waves washing over them. As we drew near, I heard another moaning from the ship as it lowered further into the sea. The tragic sound was followed by another loud crack. It was the center mast. It was falling right at us.

Before we had time to react, the mast, with its intricate rigging and shattered sails, smashed through the skiff, throwing us both into the water. When I surfaced, I was about ten feet from Daniel. He was grasping the mast.

"Dan!" I yelled. "Let's swim for it!"

A confused look came to Daniel's face. "I can't! I'm caught in the rigging!"

I turned to the other boats and waved my hands. They had seen the whole thing and one was on its way. The other went for the last few on board.

I quickly swam for the mast. When I got there, I felt around Daniel's body. The ropes were everywhere. I tried pulling them loose, but they were wound too tightly. I looked into Daniel's eyes. "I'm sure one of them has a knife. We'll cut the ropes when they get here." I turned to see the boat coming. It seemed to creep through the water. "Hurry! Hurry! He's caught in the ropes!"

The boat going for the remaining few, loaded, and was heading back to the island. All would soon be safe. As the other was some forty feet from Daniel and me, I heard another splintering crack. The vessel had shifted again, sinking lower below the waves, breaking the rear mast. It came down toward the skiff that was coming for Daniel and me. The top of the mast crushed the boat just as the crewmen jumped into the water. They started swimming for the island.

At the same instant, I heard Daniel moan in pain. I looked at him.

His eyes expressed the cutting pain around his body. "The ropes are getting tighter. I can hardly breathe." There was anguish in his voice.

I turned, screaming to the men in the water. "Come back! All I need is a knife! Come back!" My frustration was getting the best of me.

Daniel reached out and gently touched my shoulder. "Don't blame them. They're just as scared as we are." He paused for a moment, looking at me with a similar look as he had that night on the beach, when he thought I was leaving. But it was different. His eyes had that same going away expression, the pain of losing, but not for me. It was for himself. He knew it was he that was going away from me. He was the one who was leaving. He was the one who was going to die. "Jimmy . . . Swim for it. Save yourself."

My eyes darted back and forth, looking at his. A lump formed in my throat and a cold, more frigid than the icy water we were in, raced through my being. For some crazy reason, the scene from the movie *Captains Courageous* flashed in my mind. But I was not like Freddy Bartholomew. There was no one holding me back. I would not let Daniel go. I would stay with him, whatever the consequences. "No way!" I snapped back. "I'm not leaving you here alone. I don't care what happens. I'm not going until you come with me." I turned quickly to see the last boat heading for us.

Daniel put his arm around me. Doubt welled up in his eyes and his voice was calm and quiet. "If I don't make it, think of me and the good times. We had something special."

"We're going to make it! The other boat's on its way." I tried to be as gruff as I could to keep from crying. Knowing Daniel was in pain and there was the possibility he could die made my mind crazy. I turned again and yelled. "Hurry! Please hurry!"

"Jimmy." His face and voice became serene. "If something happens . . . remember I love you. I'll love you for all time. Look for me in the next life. I'll be looking for you." His mouth formed a big smile and he winked his left eye.

I saw he was serious about the dilemma. Somehow he knew he would not be coming out of this one. His face reflected a demeanor of acceptance.

"Don't think about that now. They'll be here any minute and we can cut you free." I was optimistic.

"Promise me." Daniel demanded.

"I promise . . . If something happens. But I'm not giving you up. I love you too much to let you go. We're going to be just fine." I was obstinate.

Suddenly, a scream rose from the crowd on the island. Some were helping others to higher ground and others were pointing out to sea. The men in the boat looked, too, then started rowing back to the island.

I turned to look and my heart pounded as I saw it in the distance. Daniel saw it, too.

Something deep inside me knew we were doomed. I looked into Daniel's face. I became calm. "Oh Dan, I do love you. I'll love you forever . . . Find me . . . Find me." I kissed him.

He spoke softly and tightly hugged me. "I love you, Jimmy." He peered into my face. His eyes glinted with warmth and love.

He gave me a big smile. "Goodbye, Jimmy." He winked his left eye.

I smiled. "Goodbye, Dan. Until the next life." I hugged him tightly.

In seconds, the cold, dark waters of the enormous wave came crashing over us. The light in my brain faded with the image of Daniel's face, and then went out.

CHAPTER XIII

It was pitch dark and I was aware of a subtle cool breeze on the end of my nose and the tips of my ears. My body felt weightless, like it wasn't there. I could hear a low hum. Maybe it was some distant motor. I strained to see, but I didn't know if my eyes were open. Then it dawned on me. I was dead and standing at the gates of Hell. My Hell was not going to be the 'fire and brimstone' everyone thinks of. No. Mine was going to be what I hated most. The cold. I was at the gate of my own personal Hell. A Hell of ice and snow. And the sound was that of the motors to the giant refrigeration units, somewhere far below. My mind went wild. "Dan! I can't see! I'm dead!" I yelled.

Suddenly, a hand grabbed my shoulder. A man's voice came from nowhere. "No. You're not dead. But you're pretty banged up. And the reason you can't see is because we've got the top of your head all wrapped up."

"Where's Dan and who are you?" I was lost in the dark and wanted to go home. Home to the lighthouse. Home to Daniel. But who was the unknown voice? What did he say?

"Doc Jannett. And I have no idea about Dan or where he is. Now, you will have to rest at least one more day before we can take off the bandages."

"But I have to find Dan." I tried to move. Suddenly, my body became aware of itself and the pain of the bumps and bruises hit my brain. I settled back on the bed I was in. I had no idea whether it was day or night. "I need to find out. I need to find out. Where am I? What's going on? Where's Dan?"

"You're in the hospital. You know you're pretty lucky they found you after the storm. Bob Williams knew you were out doing artwork, across from the old lighthouse. You were on the shore, at the end of the point, in the rocks."

"What about the others?"

"Others?"

"Yeah. All the people from the <u>Serenada</u>?"

"The <u>Serenada</u>?"

"The ship! The <u>Serenada</u>! Dan and I were helping the people off and bringing them to the island. They're on the island. Dan got caught in the rigging . . . Oh God!" It finally hit me. The terrible reality of it all. Daniel was gone. He was dead. My heart broke. "DAN!" The light in my head blew out.

When I came to again, I had no idea how long I'd been out. Since I knew I wasn't dead, I realized the cool breeze was the air conditioning system. The low hum was the sound of the motors, somewhere in the building. I could feel the pain again of my body. I felt like I'd been hit by a truck. The thought of Daniel's smiling face and gleaming eyes made me forget the pain for a moment. I whispered softly. "Dan."

I heard a familiar voice. "I think he's awake. Jim? Jim? It's me. Bob Williams."

"Bob? Bob? What happened?" I asked of the voice.

"Jim? Why the hell were you out there with the storm and all? I didn't see you at the opening of the show, and I got real concerned when you didn't come in the day after the judging. I know you're modest, but I knew you'd like to know if you placed. And there's that subject of eating the frame, remember? That's when I realized you'd been out painting at the lighthouse. It had to be your favorite spot. As I told you, the damn thing's in the background of all the paintings you put in the show. I told them to check. They found your car out there so I knew you had to be there. Doc said they found you just in time. If you'd been out there much longer, you might have died from your injuries and exposure. He said it was a miracle you lasted as long as you did. Listen. They're bringing the food down the hall right now. I think they'll take those damn tubes out of your arm if you'll eat something. Do you think you might be able to eat something?"

"I think I could eat a moose." I hadn't realized my hunger until Bob said something about food. I was ravenous.

"Good! Can't have my star painter starving to death."

I heard Bob leave the room for a moment. When he returned, I heard the rattle of a tray being set in front of me. The smell of fried chicken filled my nostrils. "Fried chicken? I love fried chicken."

"Well eat away, and there's more where that came from. And if there isn't, I'll run out and get you some."

I began to gobble the food like someone was going to take it away from me.

"Slow down! Slow down! It won't disappear. Nurse? Could we have several more pieces of that chicken brought up here? Thank you very much."

Then I heard the doctor's voice. "How's he doing?"

"I think he's eating you out of at least a week's worth of chicken.

Doc? Remind me never to invite him to dinner. Could be real costly." Bob laughed.

I reduced the speed at which I was consuming the food, and continued my questions. "Bob? Where did they take Dan? And what about the people on the island? There must have been some fifty of them."

"Jim. I don't know what's going on in your head. But there's a few things we need to get straight. Doc said you babbled something about the <u>Serenada</u>. Listen. You have to level with me about this whole thing, because a lot of stuff you're bringing up just doesn't make sense. Now, why don't you start from the beginning so I know what's going on."

"The storm! It was the storm!" I tried to organize my thoughts.

"Yeah. We know. Kind of freaky. It just came out of nowhere. Caught everybody by surprise. But it was quick and didn't do too much damage. It didn't even affect the opening of the show. Just a couple of folk were brought in for minor cuts and bruises. But how did you get stuck out there? Why didn't you run for higher ground?"

"We were getting the people off the ship and taking them to the island."

"The ship?" Bob's voice hesitated.

"The <u>Serenada</u>, I saw the name on the bow, just before it went under. Dan got caught in the rigging from the toppled mast. No one could get there with a knife to help. I couldn't leave him. I just couldn't. No one should have to die out there like that, all alone." I paused as my emotions began to take hold. The bandages concealed the tears in my eyes. "Dan's dead. Isn't he? Oh Bob! My friend is dead. I know he's dead."

Bob spoke quietly to calm me. "Jim. Tell me a little about Dan."

"He's the one who takes care of the lighthouse, Daniel Coffin. He's been living out there by himself since his Mom and Dad died." I thought about it. "It's strange. They died the same way." In a moment, I returned to the subject at hand. "A huge wave hit us, that's all I remember. Bob? . . . He's dead isn't he? That's why no one wants to tell me where he is."

"Jim?" Bob paused for some time. "I don't know what happened to you out there. And I don't know how to tell you. I know artists have incredible imaginations, but there's something very strange about this whole thing. Have you been to the old maritime museum up on Cline Street?"

"No." I answered calmly after gathering myself together. "But what does that have to do with all this?"

"After Doc Jannett takes your bandages off tomorrow, we'll take a run over there. Frank Neiley's the curator. I think you need to talk with him and see some of the things there. Maybe your questions might be answered."

"Okay. If you think it might help."

"See you tomorrow around ten. And by the way, congratulations are in order. The portrait you did came in Show Grand Winner. They were amazed at how life like it is. Everyone commented on the haunting eyes and the mysterious smile. And, for the first time ever, they couldn't decide which one of your others should come in First Place. So they made all your paintings First Place Winners. You've got enough blue ribbons to make a shirt. See! I told you not to worry. Don't tell me I can't recognize talent when I see it."

"Thanks Bob. I appreciate your encouragement."

CHAPTER XIV

I found out I'd been in the hospital for five days. These days were lost forever in the passage of time.

Doctor Jannett came in sometime around nine o'clock that morning and began to remove the bandages. As the last of the wrappings were coming off, Bob walked in.

"Tell me his sight's been impaired and I'll kill somebody."

"I think everything's just fine." Doc removed the last of the bandages. He looked into my eyes. "How is it?"

"No problem. I can see just fine." I picked out several items around the room, focusing on them to make sure of my hasty approval. I was correct. Everything seemed to be all right. I was not aware of any impairment.

"Well, he does look a little worse for wear." Bob commented.

"Yeah. But he'll be just fine. Those bruises should clear up in a few weeks. We'll take the stitches out of his forehead in a day or two."

I tried to smile and be pleasant, but even my face hurt. I took one look in the mirror. This gave me some idea of the facial damage. There was a bruise on my right forehead and one on my right cheekbone. The stitched cut was at the hairline on the left side. "Do you think I'll scare anyone out there, looking like this?"

Bob laughed. "I doubt it!"

A few walks across the room made it clear I hadn't lost my balancing faculties. I put on my clothes.

In thirty minutes, we were in Bob's car heading to the museum. It wasn't very far away.

When we went inside, Bob introduced me to the curator. "Frank? This is Jim Jefferies, the man I told you about. I think it might be beneficial for him to see the things on the second floor."

Frank bowed slightly and gently shook my hand. "Would you like a cup of coffee? I just made a fresh pot. While we have some, I can give you a little history that might interest you. Bob said that you were interested in the <u>Serenada</u>."

We went into a sitting room where the elderly gentleman poured us each a cup. Then he asked us to make ourselves comfortable. After a few minutes, he started his story.

"The <u>Serenada</u>, pride of the Arbash Shipping Company. A three-masted clipper of the late Nineteenth Century, sleek and graceful. Truly, first class. She was arriving from England when she got caught in a storm, just off the coast. Her captain knew if he could make the inlet, all would be safe. Just out of the inlet, the drive chain from the wheel broke, leaving the ship helpless and unable to steer. He had his men working on it immediately. Makeshift repairs were completed, and he turned to the south. Unfortunately she had drifted too near the rocks. A wave forced it onto the rocks, just south of the old lighthouse."

"Just after she hit, there was a mysterious skiff picking people from the water. No one knew where it came from, but they all were glad to see it. The two men in it helped a great number of the fifty-seven people to the safety of the island. Many of the passengers and crew applauded their courage and bravery. They indicated if it hadn't been for them and their help, many of the lives would have been lost."

"The skiff was making one last trip for the last few waiting on board when a terrible thing happened. A mast broke, falling on the two in their boat. The remaining few were saved by one of the two lifeboats launched from the ship. The other was on its way to help the men in the water, as one of the men was tangled in the downed rigging. The other man could have swam to safety, but he refused to leave his friend. As the second lifeboat approached them, another terrible thing happened. Another mast came down, smashing the lifeboat. Fearing for their lives, the men from the lifeboat struggled, swimming through the waves back to the island."

"Many of the passengers watched the tragedy unfolding. The last lifeboat headed out in an attempt to rescue them. One of the men kept calling for help for his friend. Before the lifeboat could reach them, a great wave came in from the sea. It engulfed the <u>Serenada</u>, then swept the two men into eternity. They were never found. Later, it was discovered that one of the men was the keeper of the lighthouse. They never knew the identity of the second man. No one could imagine such a tragic event. And the real irony was the loss of the two men. If they hadn't been there, the loss of life could have been significant. There was not one casualty in the disaster, except for the two men."

"Yes, as the stories from those saved emerged, the two men became more than just heroes. They became bigger than life. And what kept the story alive was the mystery. They knew who one of the men was, but could never find out about the other one. Who was he? Where did he come from? What was his name? Why was he there? Yes, it baffled everyone. Even now, these questions still haunt the town."

"All the passengers and crew as well as some of the wealthier town folk and the shipping company contributed money for the erection of a bronze plaque on a piece of black granite, honoring the memory of the two men who gave their lives for the safety of many. It sits in the rocks on the south side of the island."

"Because of the changing shipping lanes, the increased size of the more modern steam vessels and the shallowness of the inlet, the shipping company had already decided to discontinue the use of the lighthouse. The larger ships needed a bigger port and this town was destined to die as a shipping center. With less and less shipping coming to this area, the lighthouse was becoming unessential. But because the man who kept the light operating was still rather young and he had no training for anything else, the powers that be were planning to let him live out his life at the cottage, if he so desired, and pay him a monthly severance. It would be their way of retiring the lighthouse. His untimely death seemed to be a quirk of fate. And with his death, the light was never used again. The island was abandoned and turned into a memorial to the past and to the memory of those two men. The place has been treated with respect, almost like a cemetery, only the ravages of time and the elements have marred the island. Then, about three years ago, one of the relatives of the lighthouse keeper bought the island and plans to restore it to its original beauty and quaintness."

I sat listening to the story I lived just a few days earlier, but I was truly confused. "Mr. Neiley. You speak of the entire event as if it took place some time ago. I don't understand."

"Oh, but it did! The wreck of the <u>Serenada</u> took place in the late summer of 1883."

I was stunned. "That's impossible! That's over a hundred years ago! That's impossible!" I looked at Bob. "It couldn't have happened that long ago. I don't understand."

"Let me show you the rooms we've devoted to the <u>Serenada</u> and the lighthouse." Frank stood up and headed for the stairs. "Come with me."

Momentarily, we walked into the large double room. In the middle of the first was a scale model of the lighthouse. The detail work was excellent. A small label indicated the model showed how the island looked at the turn of the century.

On the walls were construction drawings for the tower and cottage. Many photos accompanied the drawings, as did several paintings and sketches of the island from the shore done by numerous artists and donated to the museum.

In the middle of the second room was a replica of the workings of the light mechanism. I examined it closely and smiled. In my mind, I could see Daniel getting it ready and setting it alight.

Around the room, against the walls were glass cases containing memorabilia going back to the late seventeen hundreds up to the present. Old tintypes of the ceremony for the dedication of the memorial plaque hung on the walls. The photographs reminded me of the ones I'd seen taken by Mathew Brady from the Civil War period.

I slowly walked around the room, looking at the pictures. Suddenly, I came to an old eight-by-ten sepia photo, hanging above a glass case. A small identification plaque beside the photo indicated it was a picture of the lighthouse keeper, taken in the summer of 1883. I smiled and touched the glass over the picture of a man, his legs apart, hands on his hips, and wearing a captain's cap. A big smile filled his face. In the distant background was the island. He was wearing a shirt with several discolorations on it.

Below the picture, in the glass display case, was the same shirt from the photo. The colors were faded, but I knew it well. "I promised I'd get him another, but I never got the chance." I whispered as tears started down my face. A card beside the shirt indicated it was the same one as in the photo, belonging to Mr. Daniel Coffin. The shirt was donated by his relatives, Mr. and Mrs. Michael Coffin of New York City.

I began to recall Daniel's odd reactions to things I told him or brought home. No wonder he didn't understand. They didn't exist yet. I shook my head, remembering when he referred to the plastic tonic bottle as flexible glass. And Rachmaninoff didn't complete the Paganini Variations until 1934. I wonder what he'd have thought if he'd ever seen my car. I wonder why he never questioned my comings and goings and how I did it? Maybe he did know about the car, but just never questioned it.

I looked at the photo again. It felt like my heart was being torn from me. I couldn't help myself and I began to sob.

Bob saw my anxiety and came over, putting his hand on my shoulder. "Are you alright?"

I pointed at the photo. "It's Dan."

Bob looked at the picture. "By God! It's the man in your portrait! But that's impossible. That painting had to have been done from life." He gave me a strange look.

I looked in the next case. There were all Dan's tools for doing his glasswork. Next to the case was the grinding wheel. Three pieces of his work were also displayed. Not his best by far. Another card was in this case indicating the items had been donated by the same Michael Coffins.

"I told him his work was museum quality. Bob, you should have seen some of his really good work. It was so beautiful."

My mind kept trying to accept the facts, but it was difficult. How could I deny an entire summer? A summer that would affect the rest of my life. How could I deny the subject of the best paintings I'd ever done? How could I deny the personality, the caring, the sensitivity, the kindness and love I shared? There had to be an answer to all this, but where could I look to find it? I turned to Bob. "I had to have been there! The proof's right here in front of me." I pointed to the shirt. "I'll explain about the shirt someday. Thanks for your help, but I know the answer must be out at the lighthouse."

"Want me to take you out there?"

"No. But thanks. I need to be alone on this one. I'll take a cab. If I don't call you by eight tonight, I'd appreciate it if you'd come out and pick me up."

"Are you sure you're going to be alright?"

CHAPTER XV

I asked Bob if I could borrow a pair of binoculars. He indicated that he had a set and would gladly let me use them. He had them at the gallery. From his gallery, he called a taxi for me to take me out to the lighthouse.

"Bob, I can't thank you enough. Maybe by this evening I may have some of my many questions answered. Who knows?"

"If you're not back before the sun goes down, I'm coming after you. Can't have something else happen to my star artist." He gave a big smile and patted me on the back as I climbed into the taxi.

The taxi driver was reluctant to drive beyond the end of the asphalt. After begging and offering him an additional twenty dollars, he took me to the end of the shell road and dropped me off.

As I walked through the dunes, I could see the top of the lighthouse tower, looming above them. My mind instantly recalled the first time I walked to the beach, surprised in the fact the lighthouse was on an island.

Within a few minutes, I stood on the beach. The sea was rather calm, with only an occasional wave breaking on the rocks.

I raised the binoculars to my eyes. Looking out across to the island, it was difficult to accept the whole thing. The slate roof of the cottage was gone, revealing the bare larger structural beams, supported by the stone outer walls. Grass and weeds grew up and around the structure. A few lonely flowers gave touches of color to the crevices and crannies in the rocks.

I stopped and focused on the front door of the cottage. It was still there, standing half-open. I smiled as I thought of seeing him there that first day.

There was something growing to the right of the door. It covered the wall, went up over the door and along the roofline. The deep green foliage accented the hundreds of cascading clusters of yellow. Could it possibly be the rose Daniel and I planted a few days earlier, a century ago? But how was that possible? There is no way the rambler could have lived this long.

Then I turned the binoculars up at the top of the tower. The metal roof was rusted in many spots and many of the glass panes were gone. Moving down the tower, I saw that many of the port windows at the second level were missing, but all those on the first seemed to be there. Except for the deterioration of the structures, everything else seemed the same. Time had no effect on the geological scale.

"WHY ME?...I DON'T DESERVE THIS!...WHY ME?" My anger was out of control.

I sat down on a nearby rock and rubbed my hand over it. It was the same one I used to sit on while waiting for Daniel to arrive in the skiff. If only the rocks could speak.

"God! What about me? It's not fair! It's just not fair!" I tried not to cry by biting my lower lip, but it didn't work. What was I going to do?

I looked at the spot where I used to set up my easel and imagined myself standing there with Daniel behind me, as he sometimes did, giving his critical comments, which were never critical. He would just tell me how great my work was.

Reminiscing about the last few months, I began to visualize the whole summer's events in my mind like a movie. I was glad to have the memories so vivid. They would give me the strength to get through the pain of losing the best thing to happen to me in my life. My rage was focused at God for taking away the only person I ever cared for and loved. Not only that, but we didn't have much time together. How could He be so cruel? I could not fathom the reason for it all. The answer had to be at the lighthouse.

The sun was warm, but suddenly there was a strange tingle in the air, like some minor electrical charge running through my whole body. Something was beckoning me. "I must get to the island. That's where the answer is. I know it's there." As I spoke, the tingling became more intense.

I stood up and removed all my clothes, except for my undershorts. I folded and placed everything on the rock where I'd been sitting and put the binoculars on top to keep everything from blowing away.

The several bumps and bruises made me question the reliability of my body. I moved my arms and legs. Although there was some aching, my curiosity and determination told me I could make it. I also remembered what my grandmother used to say. Salt seawater was good for what ails you.

It was scary at first, even though the sea was relatively calm. But once I passed the small breaking waves, all I had to deal with were the swells and twisting currents. Somewhere around the halfway point, I thought of the swim back, but quickly dismissed it. I didn't want to think about that right then.

Finally, I crawled up onto the small beach where we used to moor the boat. I chuckled to myself. Daniel would be proud of me. I sat for a time to catch my breath, then walked to the old stone steps, leading to the cottage. "Last one up's a rotten egg." I could hear and visualize Daniel and me in my mind and I sadly smiled.

When I reached the top, my first sight of the cottage's interior was through the one broken pane in the west window of the dining area. It was a miracle, but all the other panes were still in place. How they remained in the old unpainted framing was a mystery. The glass was virtually opaque from the dust, dirt and time.

I walked around to the front door. What I had seen from the shore was a rose bush. The fragrance was overwhelming. I looked at the flowers closely. They were yellow with a slight touch of pink on the edges of the petals. Could this be the same rose Daniel and I planted?

I pulled a cluster of the flowers to my nose. The electrifying tingle grew intense and I could hear Daniel's voice, like in a dream. "My love for you will keep this rose alive." The memory made me smile. It had to be the same one. I wanted to think so. "Oh, Dan. It's so beautiful." I closed my eyes and took a deep whiff of the wonderful fragrance. The next time I painted the lighthouse, I would include the rose.

I grabbed the handle of the door, opening it completely, then walked in. No longer were the warmth and coziness present, but there was still a bizarre romantic picturesqueness to the whole thing. I thought of old English landscapes of ruined buildings and churches.

Grass grew between the stones in the floor. The stairs to the loft were dilapidated and falling down. Birds had been using all the nooks and crannies of the house for nesting places.

Slowly walking through, I remembered the opening scene in the movie *Rebecca*, adapted from the book by Daphne Du Maurier.

This was not the imposing Mandaley, by any stretch of the imagination, but that same haunting quality was there.

My mind still tried to put it all together. For one fleeting moment, there was a touch of doubt. Maybe I had imagined the whole thing. Maybe it was a figment of my inner loneliness, looking for that certain someone. Maybe it was my desire to find happiness and love.

At that instant, the tingling sensation came back, stronger than ever. I continued to look around. If it was my imagination, how is it I knew where everything was in the house?

I came to the doorway to the tower. It was shut. Grabbing the handle, I pulled hard. Slowly it opened as the hinges groaned and squeaked. Walking into the dark stairway, I started up. The little niche where Dan kept his lamp was empty. I was glad the day outside was bright as the panes of the peephole windows were quite dirty, letting in very little light. My eyes quickly became accustomed to the dimness and I hurried up the steps.

There was nothing on the first landing except for the dust of time. My bare feet made the first prints there in a long time. Just as I had observed from the shore, all the windows had their glass. I had a short reverie. It was of the day when Daniel told me how he use to pretend this room was a fort. The moment of happiness passed and I started up the steps to the next landing.

The second landing was much like the first, except a great number of panes were missing from the port windows. Birds had used this area for nesting, too.

I started up the last spiral. As each step brought me closer to the light chamber, I kept wondering what I expected to find there, if anything. Would there be something that would allow me to come to grips with the matter? Would there be an answer why I somehow was permitted to step through a window in time? What was the reason? Why did I have to get wrapped up in something that would totally upset my life? Why was I allowed to find friendship and love, only to have it snatched away so quickly? Was I the brunt of some horrible time warp joke?

As I neared the top, the electrical sensation came again, this time with the impact of an earthquake. Suddenly, I started thinking in a different direction. Maybe it was for Daniel I was sent back. Maybe it was so he would have happiness and love in his life, before it so tragically ended. Maybe it WAS for him. My whole body was once again hit with the sensation.

The old light mechanism was in disrepair and nearly all the reflective mirror panels were gone. Most of the glass panes were gone in the outer wall as well. I quickly looked down at the lower section of the east wall. A glass pane was there. Could it be the same one that Daniel had made for me? I crouched down, touching the glass.

Even through the caked dirt and grime, the cut and etch work was still visible. At that moment, I knew it had all been real. It WAS for Daniel. I was sent for him. A tear ran down my cheek. My heart pounded and my body trembled. I also knew, he was gone forever.

I slowly stood. The air was intense with the sensation. I drew a deep breath, crying out his name. "DAN!" The sound rushed through the chamber, out through the metal framework, then was lost in the sea breeze. My heart ached with his loss. Hurting inside, I thought of myself. Through my crying, I whispered. "But what about me? It isn't fair to me. I've got nothing but memories. It's not fair."

The tingling grew even stronger and shocked through my body again. Suddenly, there came a voice calling from somewhere outside the light chamber. "Hello, the lighthouse!" The deep, masculine tones brought an instant recollection of the moment I first hear Daniel's voice.

I stopped crying and stood frozen, wondering what was going on now. Then it came again. "Hello the lighthouse! Hello, James Jefferies!"

My heart pounded. Was I hearing correctly or was this another trick of my imagination? I quickly tried to open the door to the catwalk, but it was rusted shut. I couldn't get out to see the ground. "DAN!" I yelled and headed for the stairs. I knew I'd be able to see out one of the broken windows on the landing below.

My mind whirled, hearing the voice over and over again. Maybe I'm losing it. Next stop the loony bin.

Reaching the landing, I ran to the broken window on the south side. My eyes raced over the visible area of the island below. There was nothing. I quickly moved to the right. There was nothing on the western side of the island either.

"James Jefferies! Are you up there?" The voice called again. It was coming from down and to the right.

I moved to where the northwestern side of the island was now clearly visible. I almost went into shock.

There, on the little beach by a small skiff, standing legs apart, hands on his hips, looking up at the broken windows, was a tall, well-tanned man, wearing sneakers, shorts and a short-sleeved shirt. His face had a square line and a black mustache, extending beyond the corners of his mouth. A captain's hat covered most of his black wavy hair. I could barely see, but his temples were slightly graying. It was Daniel.

I yelled with delight. "Dan! Wait! Don't go! Wait! I'm hurrying! Please don't go!" I ran down the steps, leaping through the dimness, trying not to fall. Within moments, I passed the first landing and was on the last spiral down.

Reaching the bottom, I catapulted through the doorway, through the dilapidated cottage and out the front door. I quickly ran to the top of the stone steps to the beach, and stopped.

My heart raced and I was breathing heavily. I looked down to the sandy beach below to make sure my eyes had not deceived me. He was still standing there, a big grin on his face. My eyes began to blur with tears. "Dan! Dan! It's you!" I started running down, wiping my eyes so I wouldn't misjudge my footing. Trying to watch my step so I wouldn't fall, I constantly yet quickly looked up to make sure the mirage did not disappear before I had a chance to reach it.

At the bottom, I started across the sand toward the figure. Suddenly, I stopped within ten feet of him. I looked directly into his eyes. At first I thought it was the tears distorting the light. But then it was clear. His eyes were not blue. They were dark brown-green. I realized it wasn't Daniel after all. The brain started again. But it looks like him. It sounds like him. I stood there somewhat embarrassed, having really made a fool of myself.

He looked me up and down, grinning. "Great swim suit you've got there." He chuckled, then he became serious. "What was that you were yelling?"

"I'm sorry. I thought. Well. It's a long story. Please forgive me. I thought you were someone I, someone I once knew." I stumbled through my words trying to say something that would make sense. Then I thought of how I looked, standing there in my slightly damp undershorts, covered with bruises and bumps.

"You ARE James Jefferies? Aren't you?" He asked politely.

I looked up into his eyes. "Yes. But I . . ."

He quickly cut me off. "The same James Jefferies, who painted the portrait at the gallery in town?"

"Yes. But I . . ."

He cut me off again. "Looks like you've been in a big fight. Hope the other guy looks as bad." He laughed. "Just kidding. But I do have several questions and things I'd like to talk to you about. Some of them might seem strange and off the wall. How about we go somewhere and have a drink and some dinner?" His voice was quiet and calm. "First, I'd like to set this wreath."

"Set the wreath?" I didn't understand.

He leaned over into the skiff and pulled up a floral wreath, almost four feet in diameter. It was made of hundreds of colorful flowers.

He just continued his commentary, not answering my question. "When you're in advertising, you're always looking for good artists. You never know when one will turn up, so you're constantly checking out art shows to see what's new. I used to come here in the spring each year to put down the wreath, but this year I heard about the art show and thought I'd kill a couple of birds with one stone. Needed to check with the contractors and also thought I'd see the art show, as well as put out the wreath."

"Did you know the show's received a great amount of publicity in the city this year? From what I understand, a lot of important people were coming from New York to see it, so I thought I might as well come, too. Bob Williams has worked real hard on its publicity."

"And speaking of Bob, I met him for the first time today. He saw me at the door of the gallery when I first walked in. His teeth almost fell out. He said something about seeing a ghost from the past. He never did explain himself real well about his shock, but he told me a little about you and showed me the portrait. Have to admit it was a bit unsettling to see yourself on canvas. But with blue eyes? And the painting done by someone you've never met?"

He smiled a warm smile. "Damn good painting. Damn good. I asked Bob if he knew how to get in touch with you. When he said you were down here at the lighthouse, I thought it a stroke of real luck, as I was coming out here anyway. It's a family tradition to put a wreath at the marker once a year. We've been doing it, seems like forever. And rightfully so! We owe them both a great deal." He kept looking at me very strangely, as if trying to make some sort of decision based on my reactions to his comments. "But we'll discuss that at dinner. I told Bob I'd bring you back to town."

I looked at the flowers. "May I help you with the wreath? It's so beautiful. And I've not seen the plaque yet."

"Sure. No problem. Come on and get in. We'll row around to the other side of the island." He kept watching my every move and expression. I seemed to be a curiosity to him.

In a while, the skiff landed on the south side of the island and we both carried the wreath to the marker. As he set the wreath in place, I looked at the bronze plaque.

It was almost two feet square with a quarter inch raised, simple border. At the top, sculpted in relief, were two left arms clasping one another just below the elbows. Below and in large letters, were the words: "Dedicated to the Memory of Daniel Coffin and his Unknown Friend." Below this were words in smaller letters. "Because of your unselfishness, bravery and love for mankind, we were all saved. One of you could have been saved, but he refused to leave the other. Because of your friendship and devotion to one another, you were both lost. May God grant you peace and may your friendship last for all eternity. We thank you both. The 57 Passengers and Crew of the <u>Serenada</u>. Lost September 5, 1883."

In my sadness, I smiled, thinking what a nice gesture this was. I was sure Daniel would be pleased.

He set the wreath with gentle care, removed his hat, and stood silent, looking at the marker. After a few moments, he spoke softly. "Thank you Cousin Dan and your friend. May you both . . ." He paused for a second, staring right at me. Then he looked back at the marker. "May you be at peace." He stood silent for a few more minutes, then put the captain's hat back atop his wavy hair.

"He was your cousin?" I asked.

"My great, great cousin to be exact, on Dad's side of the family."

"But of course, you're a Coffin! That's why you look so much like him!" I stopped short in what I was saying. He might think I'm crazy.

He looked very hard at me, after what I had just said. Then his face relaxed and he grinned, thrusting his right hand forward. "Sorry! Phillip! Phillip Coffin!" His sparkling dark eyes were warm and sincere. "Don't know why I didn't introduce myself sooner."

I recalled the day Daniel introduced himself to me, the same big grin on his face. It was funny, too, that Phillip's introduction was delayed, just as Daniel's was. Maybe this was a family trait. I returned the smile and shook his hand. "James, Jim Jefferies." It was like *deja vu* for me. I paused for a moment before asking. "Phillip? Would you mind if I took one flower from the wreath?"

He peered into my eyes. "I think it would be just fine."

I reached down, pulling one blossom. Then I climbed out onto the flat rock, from where Daniel and I used to swim. I looked out into the water and realized I was looking at the spot where it all happened. My eyes panned the area, settling on a single place in the water, some one hundred feet away, and just north of the group of rocks that destroyed the <u>Serenada</u>. It was the last place Daniel and I had been together.

I kissed the flower and threw it into the air toward the spot. I knew there was no way it could fly that far. But, suddenly, a gust of wind caught it. The blossom drifted right to the spot, landing perfectly on the rise of a swell. I smiled as tears came to my eyes. I spoke softly. "I love you, Dan. I'll love you forever." A warm feeling came over me. A feeling that everything was going to be all right. At the same instant, I felt two hands on my shoulders. I turned and looked up into Phillip's face, his hands holding my shoulders tight.

His voice was clear and calm, but there was an inquisitive intensity to it. He stared directly into my eyes. "I don't understand it all yet, and I don't know how or why. And I know it's all too impossible. But, it's YOU. It really is YOU. You are the one, the same one, and you knew him. Didn't you?"

I was shocked but also surprised that someone else seemed to be in on the secret. Someone else was searching for the pieces of the same puzzle. Had I found someone who believed the whole thing was true? Had I found someone who would listen to my story and understand? Had I found someone who could help me figure the whole thing out? Had I found someone who knew I hadn't imagined it all?

"I knew it was you the minute I saw you up close. And you haven't aged a bit. But I had to be sure. And what and how you said what you said a minute ago clinched it for me. You knew him, and . . . you loved him. You truly loved him, didn't you?" He clapped his hands together, picked me up and danced around in a circle. He began to laugh. "By tonight I'll have the whole puzzle put together. Come on! Let's go have a drink! I've got a million questions, and I'll bet you have quite a few yourself." He grabbed my arm and headed for the skiff.

I didn't understand all he was talking about, but maybe after we did talk, it would make sense. Instantly, I thought of the glass pane in the tower. "Phillip! Wait! There's one thing I'd like to get before we leave."

"What's that?" He stopped.

"Come on! I'll show you!"

We climbed the rocks to the cottage. When we reached the front door, Phillip stopped and looked at the rambling rose.

"You know, I had a botanist come look at this bush last year. I told him it had been growing here for over a century, which he found amazing unto itself. He said there is no reason on earth why it stays alive, much less in such profusion. And why it stayed on the walls? He had no answer to that either. There are no wires or rope to hold it. The wind should have blown it down a long time ago, but it hasn't. No one has an answer. Most think it's a miracle. It seems to be a real wonder." He peered into my eyes.

I said nothing. I turned and went into the ruins, leading the way to the tower. Finally, we reached the top.

"This is what I wanted to show you." I pointed at my special pane of glass in the east wall.

Phillip knelt down examining the twelve-inch square of glass.

"Now that's some fine work. Hope mine gets to be that good someday. Takes real talent to do that and not break the glass."

"You do glass work?" I was surprised.

"Yeah. Been doing it for years, on and off. Haven't done much lately though. I really should get back to it. Seems to calm the nerves, believe it or not." He chuckled.

I knelt next to Phillip, taking his huge left hand in mine, examining it. "Just like his . . . but not as rough." I felt warm in my remembrance.

Suddenly, the air was electrified and the tingling sensation was all around, as powerful as ever, filling my whole being with a strange warm feeling. I looked into Phillip's eyes.

His mouth formed a great smile and his eyes twinkled with touches of blue. "Jim! . . . . Jimmy! . . . I knew it was you. But I had to be sure. Don't you know me? It's me!"

Was I going insane? Was it a deception of the light or some bizarre breeze? I looked deeper into his eyes. A sense of joy and well being filled my entire body. It was not my imagination. I smiled.

"Yeah! It's me! Well, sort of me. It's Phillip. But I'm Phillip now. Don't you remember what I said? I told you I'd look for you in the next life. So I finally found you, and here I am! But I'm Phillip! It's too hard to explain. You'll know all about it some day. Someday far, far away. Yeah. I had to wait a long time to hit the right time and to find you. But now it's done. Gotta tell you. It's going to be great. So they told me. Wouldn't give me all the details, but they said it would all be just fine. They said we had too much love for it to have been for such a short time together. So they're giving us, well, Phillip and you, a long, long life so you can share all the things we didn't get to before. It's just so complicated to explain"

"Phillip loves you. He's known it for years, even though he's never met you. You're just what he's been looking for and needed to compliment his life. The love's been in his heart, but he's just beginning to find it out. Just give him a little time. Love him and you love me. But remember, it's his life now and I'm just part of his many past lives. But you'll know. You'll see me there. You've seen it already in his appearance, and in his eyes, even though they're brown-green. He's a good person, too. He'll treat you right. You'll see. And he really does like to do his glasswork. Get after him about it." He squeezed my hand.

"I have to let him be him again. But before I go, I want to thank you for a wonderful summer. I never knew love, until there was you. You were the one chosen to love me because you're caring and sensitive. You wouldn't allow anything to get in the way. Your sensitivity allowed you to love me, as no one else would have. And summers? We're going to have a lot more now."

"I see ya like the rose. Yeah. It's the same one. I've watched over it all this time. I did it for you." His mouth formed a big grin.

"I'm so glad I found you, Jimmy. It'll be good to be with you once more. They also said, if we're really good to one another, this time, we'll be together in the next life, too, and maybe more. I love you, Jimmy. And I won't go away from you again. We're going to have a good life. Just wait. You'll see. I am Phillip and Phillip is me. You'll understand some day. So this is not goodbye, Jimmy. It's hello…again. And remember, I will always love you, *al di la*, beyond the beyond." His white teeth showed as his grin grew wide, and he winked his left eye.

The twinkles of blue faded from his eyes, as did the tingling sensation in the air. My heart was warm and all anxiety disappeared.

I was beginning to understand. God HAD sent me for Daniel, so he would know love. But I was sure there was more to it. I felt like I was at a door and at any moment it would be opened, with all the answers pouring out. I smiled and my eyes filled with tears. Love and joy were in my heart.

Phillip's eyes glinted, the big smile still on his face. He was totally unaware of the last few minutes and of Daniel's presence. He looked at me, the tears running down my face, and a questioned look came across his. "What…What's the matter? What happened?"

I looked into his eyes. "Oh. Nothing. I'm alright." In time I would tell him of the incident that had just occurred, and he would totally understand. He would smile and hold me close, reassuring me that I would never have to worry about being loved, ever again.

"Yeah." He looked down at his large hands, with a grin. "Everybody jokes about my big hands doing tedious work like that. Maybe I'll use this pane as an example to strive toward." He stood up, extending his right hand down to help me up. "Okay! Let's go get that drink!"

"But the pane." I stated. "I'm not leaving without the pane. I don't want anything to happen to it."

"Jim! . . . Don't worry! It's not going anywhere. That pane is yours. Forever. But there's so many things popping in my mind right now. If what I say doesn't convince you, you can come back and get your pane of glass." He looked right at me. "And for some damn reason, I know I need to tell you all about them. Come on! All of a sudden, I feel like there's no time to lose."

Something told me not to worry about the pane. It would be all right.

In a flash we were at the skiff. "You sit right there." He pointed to the rear seat. "I'll row." It was funny that Phillip should ask me to sit in the same place in his boat, the same place I always sat in Daniel's.

Phillip's powerful arms thrust his boat through the water at racing speed. Soon the bow skidded onto the sandy shore.

I quickly dressed and helped put the boat on the trailer behind Phillip's four-wheel drive. As he drove to the restaurant, I combed my hair and told him of the events of the day the <u>Serenada</u> went down. By the time I finished, we had arrived.

The restaurant was very nice. Since the town catered to tourists, the casual attire was not in question. A young man was playing the piano, giving the atmosphere a cozy feeling. Phillip requested a table somewhere off in a secluded corner so we could talk without being disturbed. We sat down and the waiter came to the table.

"I'll have a whisky on the rocks . . . and Jim will have a gin and tonic. House liquor will be fine"

The waiter left the table.

I looked at Phillip. "How did you know I drink gin and tonics?"

"How do I know you drink gin and tonics? Let me see if I can tell you. Guess I'll somehow try to find a starting place." His face developed a strange look, then he smiled. It was obvious that he knew a significant part of the puzzle. A part I, too, would know very shortly. "I have to tell you." He chuckled. "The cut glass goblets have had everyone wondering for years."

"The goblets?" I questioned

"Yeah. The ones with your names on them."

"You mean they are still around?"

"You bet they are. And it's really bugged everyone forever cause no one knew who the 'JAMES' was." He chuckled. "But I really need to start from the beginning so you can follow it all. At least what I know. It'll make more sense."

"Dad's great, great, great grandfather had three sons. One was killed in the Civil War and was unmarried. One was my great, great, great grandfather. The other was Cousin Dan's father. Well. Great, great, great grandfather Setheriah was a shrewd man, into banking in New York, and had one son, Harrison, who was around the same age as Dan."

"When Dan was killed in the ship wreck, Harrison went to clear out the cottage, since the light was going to be abandoned. Setheriah was quite taken with some of the items found there, and he put them in the main vault at the bank where he was president. Then, the best thing he could do, he did. He kept his mouth shut! He also claimed Dan's bank account, which had a tidy sum built up. Needless to say, these unusual items have been a family secret since that time."

"Thomas Edison and other inventors were making the news at the time and Setheriah finally put two and two together. It was obvious that those items from the lighthouse were from some time, not his own. He didn't know how it happened, but he thought he might as well take advantage of the situation. Now as I said, Setheriah was a shrewd devil and started checking into the inventions being done at the time and waited for ones similar to the secret items. And low and behold, he invested money into these inventions by going to the inventors and telling them he would like to help back their ideas…for a profit, of course."

"Well. As time moved on, the dividends from the investments were enormous. A lot of reinvestments took place and the money kept rolling in. Then came plastics! God! It was a boom investment. What's funny is, those items have always been the family secret. Now there's so much money pouring in, we don't know what to do with it all."

"I'll bet you never thought of the impact you were going to have by leaving every day conveniences and devices from this time period back in the late nineteenth century." He began to laugh.

"I've got an advertising firm in New York, only because I wanted to do that. Money's no object! We've always felt we owed the family wealth to Dan and his friend, so the 'Wreath Tradition' began and has continued every year since. No one ever knew the how or where of the items from the lighthouse, but no one questioned the financial edge given, because of them."

"The old lighthouse has been vacant since that time. As I said, I've been putting the wreath down for several years, mainly because I wanted to do it, but three years ago, I came to the island and something got to me. Don't know what it was, but I thought it would make a terrific get away place. And with the permission of the historical society, I bought it to restore. I've been meaning to fix it up since, but never set the time aside to do it, until this year. I've hired some construction crews to start work next month. I want to build it back, just like it was, except I do want modern conveniences like running hot and cold water. With the water storage tank, a small pump, propane tank and heater, I don't see it as a problem. As for electricity, that has to all be worked out so none of the wires or whatever can be seen. I want to keep all the charm and beauty it once had. And that rose bush must be taken into account. I would like it to remain basically like it is. I love it. It adds something extra special. Now! How would you like to give me a hand with it all?"

I smiled. "Dan would be pleased, and I think it would be a lot of fun." I paused for a minute. A vision of the memory of the last day Daniel and I were together, flashed in my head. "Dan…" I paused in a slight embarrassment of something dear to my heart, suddenly being exposed. I began again. "Dan and I planted that rose on the day before he died."

"Well if I have anything to say about it, it will stay alive for another hundred years." Phillip laughed.

Suddenly, Phillip's face became serious. "Then there were the photographs. The color photographs. They knew who Cousin Dan was, but had no idea about the other fellow. And the one of Dan, in color, just like the old sepia photo in the museum on Cline Street. With the story that came out when the <u>Serenada</u> sank, they thought the other man who died with Dan, was the one in the pictures. The photos have always been locked away, as no one knew their significance."

"I saw them by accident, several years ago, when I went to the family vault. They were with the plastic soda bottles, baggies, aluminum foil, plastic wrap, TV, stereo, radio, LP records, the camera, the telephone and other things you'd left behind at the lighthouse. I was surprised to see a photo, obviously a very old photo, of someone who looked like me, and with another man. Maybe I felt closer to Cousin Dan because of them."

He paused for a moment and smiled. "I know in my heart, he was a good and kind man." He looked right at me. "And now, I sit here, looking directly at the other man in the picture." He paused for a moment. "And you knew him like no one ever knew him. You must tell me about him some day. Somehow, I feel I am like him in many ways." In time, I would discover he was more like Daniel than he could have ever imagined, not only in his physical character and movements, but in his inner qualities as well.

"The paintings, now, make sense. The six that were hanging in the cottage. They're hanging at Mom and Dad's. You'd be real pleased to see them."

"I've always admired their beauty and have tried to find information on a nineteenth century artist named James Jefferies. You see, no one connected the paintings to the secret items. So I had no idea that the one who left all the things, the one who died with Dan, the other man in the photos, and the artist were all the same person. Well, of course, there was no information on such an artist from that period. It always surprised me that someone with such talent and abilities had never been recognized."

"I used to comment that if I could find an artist as good as that, I'd hire him in a second, and he'd be head of the entire art department and right hand to me. With his abilities joined with mine, we'd have the best damn ad firm in the city, if not the country. With all that in mind, you can imagine my reaction when I walked into Bob's gallery this afternoon, and saw the portrait. There was Cousin Dan, done in the same style as the Jefferies paintings at Mom and Dad's. But what an improvement over those. This painting was alive, not to mention, still wet. Then to top it all was the signature. James Jefferies. My eyes popped out. This was impossible. My mind went crazy."

"Bob told me you'd been in an accident at the beach, getting caught in the recent storm, and that you were back at the island, trying to put some puzzle together. I knew then you were trying to put the same puzzle together that I was. I knew exactly who you were all along. Just wanted to be completely sure."

"When I got out to the land's end point, I saw your clothes on the rock, I concluded you swam to the island. I was concerned since it was rather far to swim in the condition Bob described. I put my boat in the water, and you know the rest. Now…Do you see how I knew you drank gin and tonics?"

"It's so hard to believe my visit to a remote lighthouse would have such sweeping consequences." I shook my head.

"By the way, your other paintings are incredible. But the portrait. Now that's beyond description. I know Cousin Dan was pleased." His eyes gleamed and he gave a big grin.

I sat for a moment, recalling Daniel's reaction to the painting. "He was a wonderful man and so unassuming. He felt a little embarrassed when he saw it finished, and I told him it was the face of a very handsome man. Handsome, not only on the outside, but on the inside as well."

"I was serious about the job offer, and I really want you to help with the work on the lighthouse. With you there, I know it'll be done right."

"Tomorrow I'm calling the bank to have a trust set up for you. If you're like most good artists, you're as poor as a church mouse. Not because you can't sell your work, but because you're too damn modest to take the money that's due you. From now on, you're going to have all the time in the world to paint. How does five million sound? Dan would have liked that."

"Five million? Like in dollars?" My mouth dropped open.

Phillip gleamed with happiness. "And that's just the beginning. There will be more! Lot's more! I can hardly wait for you to meet Mom and Dad. They're going to flip! Well? What do you say? Maybe you'd like to eat first before saying?"

I was so flabbergasted, I could hardly speak. "I don't know what to say. I mean . . ." I paused for a moment, then gave Phillip a big grin. "Could I borrow five dollars against my future windfall? I feel extravagant and want the pianist to play something special."

Phillip reached in his pocket and pulled out a ten-dollar bill. "Be really extravagant." He chuckled.

I walked over to the man at the piano, telling him how accomplished he was and how much I was enjoying the light classical music he was playing. The piece I requested seemed well within his capabilities. He thanked me for my generosity as I placed the bill in his glass. I returned to my seat.

"What did you ask for?" Phillip was curious.

"Something that has great meaning to me." I spoke softly.

Within moments, the notes began to sing from the piano. Never had I heard it played so beautifully and so full.

"That's my favorite piece of music." Phillip said quietly. "Ever since I first heard it years ago. It makes something deep inside me feel warm and at ease. It takes me to a place calm and peaceful, someplace far, far away. And what's so stupid is, I can never remember what it's called."

"It's the Eighteenth Variation of Rachmaninoff's 'Rhapsody on a Theme of Paganini'."

As Phillip had been talking, I'd listened and watched. It was becoming absolutely crystal clear. Now, I totally understood. God, in all His infinite wisdom, was not cruel after all. The intertwining of our three lives, as well as the interconnecting of the centuries, was all part of His grand scheme. It was His way of proving that love knows no boundaries and no time.

I quietly said a prayer telling God how sorry I was for being so hateful in not understanding. I should have known He intended it all to work out.

Phillip looked at me strangely. His dark eyes glinted in the candlelight. "I like you, Jimmy. Do you mind if I call you Jimmy? I don't know how to explain my feelings right now, but you and I have some haunting connection, a strange umbilical cord I cannot define. Somehow, I know we're going to do great things together." He lifted his glass.

I raised mine to his. The crystal goblets rang as they touched. I smiled and looked into his eyes. I could see the caring, kind and sincere man shining within. Phillip was one of the truly handsome people. Happiness filled my heart. Something deep inside me was saying I would never be alone again.

There was a momentary silence. The only sound was the piano playing the melodic theme.

Phillip's voice was clear and warm. "To a new friend." His face beamed with a wide, wonderful smile. A second later, he winked his left eye.

THE END

IN DEDICATION

**This book is dedicated first of all: to my friend,
Phillip McDonald.**

**Without him, this story could never have been
written.**

Second: to my friend, Tristrum Coffin, whose wonderful laugh brought a joy to my soul.

Third: to my friend, Danny Glass, whose trust and help have pulled me through a lot of bad times.

****

Both Tris and Dan helped me find and understand the meaning of true friendship.

And last but not least: to my friend, Seth Feinberg, who gave me a wonderful gift. He made me realize and understand I could love again.